DIALOGUES
AMONG THE
SPECIES

Patrick Conley

authorHOUSE®

AuthorHouse™
1663 Liberty Drive
Bloomington, IN 47403
www.authorhouse.com
Phone: 833-262-8899

Published by AuthorHouse 01/14/2022

ISBN: 978-1-6655-4888-5 (sc)
ISBN: 978-1-6655-4887-8 (e)

CONTENTS

A FOREWORD AND
A FOREWARNING

All characters in this work are fictitious; accordingly, anyone looking for resemblances to living or deceased beings, human or otherwise, will be disappointed. Fiction allows us an escape from reality and a retreat from the mundane even as it teases us into believing, if only momentarily, that this world of letters is real. However, if the characters and situations remain as flights of imagination, perhaps the story itself may depict some small element of truth.

DEDICATION & A NOTE OF GRATITUDE

None of this tale would have been even fictionally possible were it not for the groundbreaking work of the famed zoo-linguist, Dlorah Yelnoc. In his pre-mortem life, Professor Yelnoc devoted his considerable energies and passions to the study of communication among mammalian species, such as humpback whales and great apes. Then, when he passed onto purgatory, he and Phil worked as a team to develop an inter-species language so that all of God's creatures could talk with each other. As a corollary, they could also develop reasoning capabilities even superior to that of human beings. Only by Professor Yelnoc's and Phil's work could this and similar tales have been told.

On a personal note, Dlorah Yelnoc's passion for literature inspired his students and his children to continue his legacy by telling their own tales and writing their own books.

INITIAL CONTACT

MOST OF YOU OUT THERE don't know me although at one time I enjoyed something of a cult following. Back in the day when magazines were in their heyday, I even got featured in all the big time mags. Yeah, and who wouldda thought that an orphan from remote Africa wouldda made it so big? But you know, the crowd and fame itself is fickle. *Fama fugit* as they say. Yeah, I like to toss in a little Latin here and there just to sound intellectual although Latin is fading, too, as a sign of education. So, in all matters, human and animal, Fama fugit. But, forgive me. I failed to introduce myself properly. Call me Phil because that's the name I go by in the human world although I am not and never was human. Sometimes that's a blessing. No, I'm Phil the Gorilla. During my earthly existence, I weighed in well over six hundred pounds and could devour as much produce as was contained in a Mom and Pop grocery store. I couldn't stomach what the mega-grocery stores have on hand nowadays, but back then I was a giant among gorillas and humans. Then I went on what the newspapers called a hunger strike but it really wasn't a strike. I just got to the point where food no longer interested me. Then finally I died. The humans stuffed my body and put me on display; so popular was I that I had a flock of followers even after death. But now that fleeting fame is passing, too. My admirers have grandchildren now and these grandchildren never saw me in my prime, craftily and furtively splashing the humans who taunted me in my cage. Even then, when the humans called me a monkey and tried to goad and belittle me by jumping up and down and scratching their sides. I'm not a monkey. I'm a great ape. But a lot of the humans never got it. Anyway, after a long day of entertaining the human riff raff and even the nice humans who pitied me sitting stoically behind steel bars and bare concrete floors, I liked to split a Budweiser with my trainer who was a hell of a nice guy and understood me better than the rest of the humans. I still like to down a few ounces of the frothy drink when I re-assume material form.

And that leads me to my present stage. Even in death, I keep active. You see, I get assignments from time to time to deal with humans, many of whom are chained in by their own egos. Sometimes, the humans get so self-important and self-concerned that they need to be shaken up a bit and who better to do that than a 600+ pound gorilla? I kinda get a kick out of these post-mortem assignments. The tables get turned and the gorilla gets to teach the humans. Sometimes my students learn and sometimes they don't. But I do my best even if my pedagogical techniques are a little bit out of the ordinary. Any way, the other day I got this special assignment although in eternity it's hard to talk about the other day. Maybe I've always had this special assignment. As I was sitting down in a lush field, just soaking up the rays of sun and of divine grace, out of nowhere old Gabe comes rushing in, You always know something's up when Gabe comes swooping down, faster than an eagle and even faster than a lightening bolt. So, I readied myself for what I knew was coming: a special assignment. Actually, I don't mind these special assignments at all. They keep my mind sharp and give a chance to resupply my stock of Budweiser.

Old Gabe lands six feet away from me (even in the afterlife we sometimes got to maintain social distance although I don't know why). Then he trumpets out, "Phil, I got a job for you."

"I figured that, Gabe. So, what is it? Do I act solo or do I assemble a small convocation of my animal brethren?"

"This is a group project, Phil. But you're in charge and get to make the calls. You might need to confer with some colleagues, though, to guide your decisions. This will be a tricky and difficult assignment."

When I heard this, I sort of puffed up and almost got to chest thumping. I felt sorta proud, getting the tough jobs and all. It lets me know that the Big Boss has confidence in me. "OK, do I get to pick my team?" I glanced up at Gabe and shot him a look that made my question more of an exclamation. Don't get me wrong. Gabe is the best messenger there ever has been, but sometimes he does more than just deliver messages, if you know what I mean. Even in the afterlife, there's a certain amount of hustling and bustling to get to the top of the pecking order, and, as an archangel, old Gabe is at the top. Still, I like to make sure that I got my independence and even just a shade of pride.

"You get to choose, but—only with my approval." Ole Gabe could play the peckin' order game, too.

So, I rubbed my chin as if I were trying to settle all types of options swirling around in my head. Actually, my first pick was an easy one, but I had to play the game so Ole Gabe would approve. "Well, I was tossing around a lot of possibilities and even more candidates for my first pick. But I think Amanda the poodle, would be my first choice. She's got a level head and would keep me from doing anything rash and just plain stupid."

"A good choice. You recognize your strengths and weaknesses. Now go on."

"Well, Gabe, I need more info on what type of human I'll be dealing with before I round out my team."

"A fair request. You'll be dealing with Adam Albright, a successful—too successful—lawyer who has lost sight of what it means to be human. He thinks he's the image of perfection and can do no wrong. But he has done plenty of wrong. It's too bad. He had the best education, the best opportunities, and enjoyed success after success. But prosperity and success have blinded him."

"The kind of guy who was born on third base and has convinced himself that he hit a triple to get there," Phil observed, stroking his chin.

"You're batting a thousand so far, Phil."

"Well, considering who we're dealing with, I think that maybe Sly, the street-smart raccoon, would be my second choice."

"You realize that Sly is on probation? He's his own worst enemy and gets himself into trouble all of the time."

"You're right, Gabe. You're always right." I had to say this. Even an archangel isn't immune from a little flattery. Besides, it's pretty much the truth. I've never known Gabe to be wrong. It's just that sometimes he gets to verge on being a little overbearing. "You're spot on about Sly.

But it takes a shyster to know a shyster, and Sly is the shyster of shysters. I think that Amanda would keep him in control. A lot of people don't know this, but poodles are hunting dogs, and, if there's one thing that even post-mortem, Sly fears, it's a good hunting dog. Sly still has flashbacks to the time he got treed and shot, with a pack of yelping dogs waiting his fall. Sly will give us insight into the mind of a hustler. He will anticipate what this Adam guy will think."

"Well, Phil, if what you say is on target about Sly, perhaps you might want to consider your pick of dogs. Wouldn't a Redbone Coonhound be a better choice than Amanda, the poodle?"

"That thought did cross my mind, but I quickly dismissed it. Amanda has the right blend of gentle coaxing and, when necessary, fierce barking that she will keep Sly on a short leash. Most of the time, she can keep Sly in line with just a fixed glare that lets him know who's in charge. A Coonhound would just send Sly packing."

"OK, Phil, as long as Amanda can keep him in check. Who is your third choice?"

"Well, I was considering, Pete, the Possum. Pete was and is a material guy, and I'm guessing that this Adam fellow is, too. But I just don't think he'd have insights into a predator kind of human, the kind who likes to be the king of the hill."

"Perhaps, the king of the swamp would be a better choice."

"Who do you have in mind, Gabe?"

"Al, a sixteen foot king of the bayous, at least that's what he was in his pre-mortem life. He got to be king of the swamp by being more ruthless than anyone. He even ate his own offspring just to satisfy his gut and lust for power."

"Then how did he get into this purgatory-style afterlife for deceased animals? Shouldn't he, you know, be suffering the torments of you know what?"

"He was only following the sometimes cruel dictates of Nature, Phil. He was the best of the worst. He and Adam should get along well. They both think the same way."

Gabe had a point I had to admit. Pete, the Possum, wouldn't be much help dealing with an apex predator-type. "OK, Gabe, I'll take on Al, but on one condition. If he doesn't work out and do something stupid like threaten Amanda or Sly, he's on. Agreed?"

"Fair enough, Phil. Now you can pick one more."

"Right, Gabe. More than five in a group makes it too hard to get anything done. Well, in that case, I want Carrie, the vulture. She keeps everyone mindful of the final reality of pre-mortem life."

"All right, Phil, you've got you group. I'll go whisk away and visit each one of them to let them know of their new assignment. Amanda, Sly, and Carrie have worked with you before, so I don't anticipate any objections. I'm not so sure about Al. I'll get back to you later."

"In the meantime, I'll scout out this Adam guy's place. You know a lot about a guy when, unannounced, you scout out his place." I waited a few minutes or whatever short time in eternity is called to make sure that Gabe was off. It's not like I don't like the guy. I mean he's an archangel and all, but I just don't want somebody looking over my back when I'm reconnoitering, you know what I mean. All clear. Humans think they've got it made with GPS and all, but all I have to do is to think hard enough and puff I arrive where I want to be although sometimes that threshold between the Time / Eternity boundary can make for a bumpy ride. I got to thinking: where should I investigate first. Adam lived in a swanky part of town as you might suspect a successful predator would. In a lot of respects, his domain differed little from that of other successful predators in the human world: the same expansive front lawn, carefully manicured by immigrant labor, sort of like a medieval manor or a Roman villa. Only the workers weren't called serfs or slaves. Anyway, in that respect, all of the homes within this gated community resembled each other. It's true that the architecture of each home differed. Some called to mind colonial plantations, others Italian villas, others British estates with elaborate gardens, still others retained features of Frank Lloyd Wright's organic architecture. Adam Albright's domicile reflected the latter: low perpendicular angles that seemed nestled in the rolling fields with a superabundance of windows to let in the sun. I wanted to know what had impelled old Adam to select this type. After a little researching in our files, I found out that Adam had won this ritzy estate in a poker game. Well, not exactly. The guy who owned it ahead of Adam had gone busted and was deeply in debt. After a few too many Scotch and sodas, he dreamed of recouping his losses in a high stakes poker game. Because of the boozy miasma of his brain, he lost it all and was drowning in debt. So, Adam snatched at the opportunity to take one man's loss for his gain. He offered to assume the guy's debt (totaling some two million dollars) if the debtor would hand over his house (probably worth closer to three million) but that was ten years ago and since then real estate prices have, as they say, gone through the roof. Which is another one of those bizarre human expressions. I mean, who wants a place if something has gone through its roof. Anyway, Adam got the place and spruced it up a bit even though he didn't plant any trees—another wacko human expression. Still drowning in an alcoholic haze, the guy signed over the deed, duly notarized by one of Adam's buddies.

So, the grounds and exterior of the house exuded wealth. I've heard it said that a lot of wealthy humans spend their dough (another odd expression) on bathrooms and kitchens, so I thought I'd take a look. Adam's kitchen was all oak and stainless steel except for the marble tops. The burners (although I couldn't see any flames on the glass like tops) and oven were centered in the room with lots of pots, pans, and other utensils hanging down within easy reach. But the utensils were too clean if you know what I mean. They looked as if they had been taken out f the box and never or very seldom used. Off to the side was a rustic looking redwood table with redwood benches along the sides and redwood chairs at either end, I guess for the king and his queen of the moment. Oh, I forgot to mention that old Adam had been divorced for some time and entertained a succession of wives of the moment in his bedroom. He did have a door off to the right of his dining table. The massive oak door led to his extensive wine cellar. It looked as if it got far more use than any of the cooking utensils. But I sort of expected that. Adam was a guy who profited from his victims' fondness for booze. So, he always had a plentiful stock of alcohol on hand. On the other side of the kitchen stood a bar, also plentifully stocked. Beyond the kitchen, lay the family room although Adam's current family stood at one. None of his children visited him. Likewise, he seldom visited them except on Christmas when he dutifully played Santa Claus to his daughter, Cassie who was turning nineteen, and his son Mike, who was a senior in high school. Adam made a point of demanding that he be included on all mailings about the education of his two children but never bothered to read them. While Cassie and Mike were in high school, he made a grand appearance at the school's Open House and warmly greeted each one of his children's teachers. After that gesture, he never showed any interest until the day of Cassie's high school graduation, where he beamed at his daughter's academic and athletic accomplishments. "You must be so proud," person after person congratulated Adam. And he was. He always was. Of course, his ex-wife Mary DeLuca had been the one to check the homework, drive them to practices, and make sure that her children were always prepared. It wouldn't look good for a lawyer to be delinquent on his court determined childcare duties. On the legal documents, Adam enjoyed joint custody, but his idea of that focused on writing a monthly check and showering his offspring with material goodies on Christmas, their birthdays (His secretary always took care of the birthdays as Adam was likely to forget them), and other special occasions. So, all in all, Adam's minor estate confirmed what was already in the book. Yeah, there's a book on Adam and I had to read it as I spied on his territory.

What the book didn't prepare me for was Adam's bathroom. I sortta expected the seldom used luxury kitchen—Adam was a bachelor—and I sortta expected the wine cellar bit and the bar. But nothing prepared me for the bathroom. Not that there were gold handles or anything, but the walk-in shower alone was immense: ten feet long and five feet wide. In the middle of it lay a stainless steel table over six feet long and three feet wide. On the side against the back wall stood a mattress that was really like one of those foam swim mattresses, pink. Above, six showerheads were beamed at the table. On the ceiling, a mirror looked down on the proceedings. I guess that the shower doubled as a bedroom. So, since the bathroom seemed to be the center of Adam's life, I decided that I would initiate contact with Adam there.

But, before I had that contact, I needed to hear Gabe's report on his visit with Al. I didn't have to wait long. As if reading my mind—which Gabe probably did—he appeared instantly. "Al will be a good fit, Phil. I found him lounging in the swamplands of eternity, where he rehearsed kills—not that he needed to kill for food anymore. But, as Al

7

explained, he needed to keep his mind sharp. He said that he had come to enjoy the mental aspect of the hunt more than the actual chowing down part. And, yeah, he'd welcome the chance to offer some insight into the habits of a predator type. He said that in his pre-mortem days, he had never tasted lawyer, so he might not be able to fully digest the species, *Advocatus Hostilis,* but as one predator to another, he could provide some insight. I told him that this Adam guy seemed especially fond of creating an environment for an easy kill, and Al said he could appreciate that approach. So, Phil, it looks as if you're all set. I also messaged Amanda, Sly, and Carrie, and they all looked forward to the challenge. Sly even read synopsis of Adam's bio, bragging that he could have read the full biography but had better things to do although I wasn't sure what these better things were. Anyway, you're all set, Phil. Go ahead and initiate contact." Then Gabe was spirited away, which was fine with me because I needed to figure out the best setting for the meeting of the minds. I didn't expect things to go well.

Things didn't go well. I figured that the Bathroom would be the best place for the contact. I wanted to surprise Adam, shake him up, so that he might be open to listening to some advice. So, I figured I'd appear in the mirror while he was shaving. He'd have to confront my gargantuan, hairy face and would be frightened into reason. He wasn't.

"Who the hell are you?" Adam bellowed. Then he recovered. "I've got to cut down on snorting coke after I've had a few drinks."

"Adam, listen to me. This is no hallucination although you'd be better off staying sober enough to listen. Then you might actually listen to what I've got to say. You've got time to turn things around."

"Why the hell would I do that? Things are going my way as they always do."

"But that won't always be the case."

"Yeah, yeah, so now you're going to pull the whole Dickens' thing. So whatta you going to do? Tell me that three apparitions will come and then I'll do a 180 and be the choirboy my Mom always wanted me to be. Yeah, right, this is so nineteenth century. And as for you, you need a haircut. I'll give you the name of my own personal barber."

When Adam smarted off like that, I wanted to give him a full dose of my thundering chest thumping. And I did. He just laughed the whole thing off and wiped the mirror clean with a towel. "Enough of this BS," Adam concluded, and then he finished shaving and wiped his face clean. So I appeared full person. And then he laughed it all off as he just stepped right through me. "Subpoenas and warrants may rattle my nerves, but druggy dreams will never upset me."

To tackle this dude, I'd need some help. So, I called for a council of the five: me, Amanda, Sly, Al, and Carrie.

A COUNCIL OF THE FIVE

WELL, I HADN'T ELICITED MUCH reaction from Adam Albright, but I guess I shouldn't have expected to, either. Still, I had secretly hoped that I might have shaken him just a little bit. Yeah, yeah, I know that I shouldn't let ego get in the way of accomplishing my mission. Still, I get a kick out of seeing situations reversed. Now, I'm supposed to be the one in charge, not the humans. You know, maybe that thought will help me out a bit. In my early, pre-mortem days, the humans figured that they could pretty much treat me the way they wished: pen me up, make me the object of gawking middle school aged boys, treat me like one of those unfortunate exhibits in a circus freak show. But back then, I showed them who was boss. I'd wait, putting up with their childish antics and then slowly, ever so slowly, ease my way over to the pool in my cage, and before they could stop their gawking, splash them away and drown their illusions of superiority. Then, just as slowly as I had made my way from underneath the fake tree over to the pool, I'd make my way back to the shelter, if you want to call it that, of that same old fake tree as if nothing had happened. I gained a little respect for doing that, even some admiration. Yeah, I need to ease up, take the whole matter more slowly, gain a few minor victories, and not expect a dramatic success right away. Besides, I've got re-enforcements, my four councilors. Yeah, I've got to plan that first meeting very carefully.

You know what they say: location, location, location. The setting for our little ad hoc committee will set the tone. I didn't have to worry about the weather. In our post-mortem world, the temperature is always pleasant although it varies depending upon the species. We animals always like to meet outdoors and our assembly points always take place in the open, but not always during the day. A lot of us are nocturnal, maybe to get away from predators like humans. Deer, for instance, like to assemble at night for the most part. But, since I don't have any deer to worry about we'll meet during the day. Sly, the raccoon, might like to meet at night as most of his shenanigans occur at night, but it's best to keep an eye out on him just in case he decides to act up. For the most part, Sly isn't evil, just thoughtless and rambunctious, and a bit ornery and self-centered. No, we'll meet during the daylight hours. Amanda will be fine meeting anywhere, so will Carrie, who can swoop down from the skies any time she wishes. As for Al, the alligator, night or day makes no difference. He can sleep and swim and plan his modes of attack night or day. But I guess we ought to meet poolside out of consideration for him. If he wishes, he can always slip out of the water and sun himself on the banks of a lake, or he can immerse himself in the water with only his eyes and nostrils above the waterline.

So, it's settled. Our first and probably all of our meetings will take place by the banks of a lake. I know just the place. The lake itself is moderately large, about thirty acres in size. On the south shore, three limestone blocks about ten feet long and three feet wide create a kind of natural stairway. Then the bank itself extends about another thirty yards of close-cropped grass (although I don't know who does the mowing—maybe humans who are working off the sins of their youth in purgatory). Anyway, we can sit lakeside if we wish or spread out on the grass. Carrie will have plenty of room to land from the sky and Sly can slip into the lake for a quick dip or just sit on the ledge and wash his hands. On either side of the limestone ledges, large cattails about four to five feet high screen us off from curious onlookers. Yeah, this will be the place. To make matters official, I'll ask Gabe to message each one of my fellow councilors. You know, it's hard to talk about time when you're dealing with eternity. We're so used to doing everything by the clock. In our pre-mortem days, it seems that so much is determined by the clock—especially when you're living in a zoo. Feeding times are the same every day: 930 am and 4:30 pm. The crowds of humans come in between 9 and 5 almost every day—except for a couple of human holidays. It was pretty much the same old, same old. Now, in eternity we live in an everlasting present except on those special occasions when we have to adjust ourselves back to the demands of living in time like when we are called to special duties to deal with humans. Then we sort of drift back into human time for a spell. And for an instant, we're back to living in a chronometric environment. Yeah, it's weird all right, but that's the way the Big Boss wants it.

So, we met at morning just when the sun rose about thirty degrees above us. Al had been hanging around on the grassy area just beyond the limestone outcroppings; but, when I lumbered in, he stealthily slipped into the cool water of the lake, allowing only his nostrils and eyes to rest above the waterline.

"Hey, Al, I mean I guess you're Al as we haven't been formally introduced, there's no need to steal away into the lake. You're welcome to stay here with the rest of us."

"Just old habits, I guess, Phil—you've gotta be Phil, right?" I nodded in response. "Well, I feel more comfortable here. I understand that you've got a dog, a raccoon, and a turkey vulture who'll be joining us. I don't think that the dog or the raccoon would feel very comfortable hangin' around me, especially the raccoon. I've chomped down many a time on an unwary 'coon in the old days, so in the interest of group harmony and all that, I'll just hang around here, and let the cool waters of the lake keep me mellow. Is that OK, big guy?"

"Works for me, Al. I just don't want you to feel left out."

"No problem, Phil. I always make my presence known if you know what I mean."

Then in sauntered Amanda, precisely three minutes early. I sort of expected that. She had made a habit of always being punctual. Amanda greeted me and took a seat on the ground to my right. Two minutes later down swooped Carrie, giving a nod of recognition to Al. Carrie explained to Phil her relationship with Al. "Back in the former life, Al and I would work in tandem: he'd get first pick, I'd get the second course."

When Carrie mentioned this relationship, Al slowly turned his whole body towards Amanda and said almost apologetically, "We don't mean to offend. It's Amanda, right? I mean, you know how it was back then."

"No offense taken, Al. That was the way of Nature, and Nature can be very cruel sometime. I've known a few dogs who would toy with a rabbit they had caught in their teeth. There was no escape from those canines and incisors. Still, they'd toss the rabbit in the air a few inches and then catch it and shake it and then repeat the process. It's the way of Nature. Now we follow a different law. Well, at least most of us do."

In crept Sly, worn out from a night of foraging for food he didn't need. Still, the old habits die slowly. However, one trait stayed true to Sly's nature. Just as Amanda was habitually early, Sly was habitually late. He appeared bleary-eyed and peevish, but shot an alarmed look at Al, who lay lurking in the water. "Who's the new guy?" Sly demanded to know.

"Forgive me, Sly. Let me introduce you to Al, the newest member of our little convocation." I tried to come off as patriarchal as I could.

"What's wrong with Pete, the opossum. I like workin' with old Pete. He and I come across as a team, you know, a kind of comic duo."

"Pete's been assigned other tasks. And Al has the special instincts to give some instinct on a human predator," I added.

"I know all about those human predator types, Phil. You know I ended my earthly days treed with yelping hound below cheerin' on my demise. Then the humans took out their rifles and blew me into eternity."

"Well, Sly, then the two of us shared the same fate," Al intervened.

"What do you mean?" a startled Sly responded.

"Back in the day, I was the king of the swamp, sixteen feet of killing power. Then I got careless and took a snap at a skinned chicken that was hangin' just at the waterline. I shouldda known better. I mean, how many skinned chickens would you expect to find in the swamp. But, as I said I got careless and a little arrogant. So I chomped down not only on the chicken but a steel hook. I thrashed about at first but then settled in, tryin' to figure out how to get out of my predicament. And get out I did, but not in the way I had expected. A couppla hours later, two humans in a boat drifted towards me. One of the humans started pullin' on the line; the other one took out a rifle and aimed it at the dark figure that was slowly comin' up. Then I started thrashin' and rollin'. But too late. The human with the rifle took aim and that was it. Well, that was almost it. I got featured on one of the human TV shows as the monster gator. I almost swamped the boat of the two human hunters, who just grinned in triumph. So, I sortta empathize with your plight, Sly."

Sly nodded and raised a paw in salute as if he had met an equal. Actually, Al was more than an equal, but Sly would have to find out that for himself.

Amanda got us back on topic. "In Nature, we were all, well, almost all predators, just like the humans. Phil here was no predator, but I wouldn't want to get him riled up and angry with me. Carrie saw what damage predators could do. But that was back then. Phil, I understand that you called us together to deal with a human predator. Just what did this Adam guy hunt?'

Relieved that we had finally gotten around to the topic of our inquiry, I responded in a flat objective way. "Adam hunts for money and for sex."

At the word *sex*, Sly's ears perked up and he grinned in a salacious way. "Now it's getting' interesting. All right, Phil let's get to the sex part. I know that all humans hunt for money, but I really hadn't figured on the sex angle."

"In due time, Sly, in due time. First I need to read you synopsis of Adam's life from the big book we've got on him."

"How do we know your synopsis of the synopsis is accurate?" Sly asked. At this comment Amanda rolled her eyes, Carrie flapped her wings, and Al submerged himself completely in the water.

"Well, Sly, if you don't trust me, you're welcome to read the whole book on Adam as I have. It runs over two thousand pages."

"That's all right. I guess we can rely on you. I mean, it's not as if we have a choice or anything." Then Sly ambled over to the lake and washed his hands, all the while keeping his eyes on Al.

"That's all right, pal," Al almost whispered. "I won't hurt you. I mean, after all, we're like on the same team now. But I will tell ya that a little reading' wouldn't hurt ya." Sly didn't respond; he just rubbed his paws together frenziedly.

When Sly had finished, he ambled over to the rest of the group, but kept his distance not only from Al but also from Amanda, Carrie, and most of all from me.

Rubbing my chin, I quickly surveyed the group and then related how Adam had won his estate from a drunk in a poker game.

Amanda tried to muffle her voice but couldn't restrain her fury. "What was wrong with other humans who were playing that card game? Didn't at least one of them object? It just doesn't seem right to prey upon someone's weakness even if that weakness was the person's own fault."

"This guy Adam is what you call an opportunistic predator, right, Phil." Al intoned as if speaking from very personal experience. "He's the kind of hunter who makes sure he doesn't put himself at risk. He'll go for the easy kill and pass over potentially dangerous encounters."

"Al's right," I observed. I thought to myself that any initial doubts about including Al on the team vanished. "Let me relate a little anecdote that I think brings out a lot about Adams' character. One evening, he was at what the humans call a cocktail party. You know that word cocktail has an interesting etymology."

"OK, Phil, you can stop showing off your knowledge," Sly objected. "Just what the hell does *et-o-mogy* mean?"

"It means the origin of the word or phrase, you know where it came from," I responded, trying hard not to come off as exasperated. I knew Sly knew what the term meant. As usual, he was just trying to stir things up. "Some say the term originated from the custom of giving a horse of mixed breed a docked tail that looked like a cock's comb. So a mixed drink, alcohol and some other beverage, was called a cock's tail. Later the term was slightly simplified to cocktail."

"Yeah, right, Phil, if you say so," Sly spit back. I didn't respond because later Sly's insight into Adam's little tricks would come in handy.

"As I was saying, at this cocktail party, Adam was on the prowl, looking for some impaired person to cheat and / or seduce. One of his cronies, who strangely enough was named Guy, asked Adam why he hadn't gone into politics. Adam took him aside and explained that he didn't want to mess with all the public scrutiny, especially that business about disclosing his tax records. He was making way more money than any politician ever did—at least officially. "We all know," Adam declared, "that it's hard to figure how much some of the politicos make on the sly. Still, my lobbying pay in dollars and perks is far too imposing to give up. Naw, it's best to lie low in the swamp and just snatch the easy paychecks that drift in my way."

"I thought that that would be the case," Al declared.

"As it was with money, so was it with sex," I resumed.

"Wait, what are you telling us, Phil," Amanda demanded to know.

Carrie flapped her wings and responded. "He would feast on corpses that weren't dead but might as well be."

"Carrie, what are you talking about" Amanda asked.

"Amanda, sometimes you floor me, Sly intervened. "The guy waits until the woman he's hunting almost passes out. Then he has his way with her. The gal can't be so drunk that she can't remember, just drunk enough that any inhibitions are gone so she thinks she's made a choice when in reality the booze make the choice. That way old Adam can't be accused of rape."

"How do you know all this, Sly?" Amanda wanted to know.

"Oh, you know me. I get around at night. Sometimes I just watch the humans make fun of themselves and act worse than any animal ever would. It's a blast. I'm what they call a voyeur and specialist in humans' bad behavior. Humans watch TV and movies; I watch them. They're fools who amuse me. What egotistical imbeciles!"

Al was listening intently and said just loud enough for me to hear before he submerged completely, "It takes one to know one."

OBSERVATIONS ON HUMAN BEHAVIOR

I NEED TO DEBRIEF THAT FIRST session. Al is going to work out all right. I had my doubts at first, but Al doesn't mince words. Amanda is well, Amanda. She has a sense of rectitude about her and serves as a counterpart to Sly's antics. Carrie serves as a memento mori. Despite his self-centeredness, Sly makes a good case. Some angel, whose name I can't remember, wrote the book on Adam Albright, and is still writing it. So there's one filter. Then I read the book and delivered my synopsis of it. So, that's two filters. We try our best, but I probably missed some important things, so did the angel author of the book. We've got only part of the picture. We're mainly right, but my fellow members of the council need to see Adam in action and come to their own conclusions. Yeah, I've got to ask Gabe if we can hold a little observation party or two.

"Did you call my name?" Gabe asked ushering himself in like the west wind.

"Well, I didn't make a formal request, but now that you mention it, I guess I'd have to say that I did. That is, if it's OK with you."

"Nothing could make me happier, and the Big Guy is pleased that you're humble enough to admit that you don't have all of the answers. None of us lesser beings do. Well, enough of that. I'm no philosopher, only a messenger. But let me make a suggestion. I have it on the highest authority that the best opportunity to observe Adam in his native habitat, stalking his prey, searching for his mate of the moment would occur next Saturday night at his law firm's soiree that doubled as a campaign rally for a senator. This particular congressman had accepted so many 'gifts' from Adam that he was, as they say, neatly tucked away in the hidden creases of Adam's pocket. What if your next council consists of an observation of those proceedings? You can debrief them later on. All you'll do this session is observe."

"I like it, Gabe, but I doubt that some of my colleagues will be able to keep their thoughts to themselves. I'll wager that Amanda will be outraged at times and that Sly will admire a fellow hustler."

"No problem, Phil, it would be unnatural to demand total silence, and even in the afterlife all of you retain some traces of your pre-mortem natures. Just try to keep the focus on observation and remind everyone that there will come a time for judgment later on when all can benefit from assessing all of the individual observations. Phil, I'll go and inform the others in your little convocation of the time and nature of your next session."

"Great, Gabe, it looks as if we've got a plan." Gabe is right, I thought to myself, still he doesn't have to keep someone like Sly in line. I bet he grumbles about having his Saturday night interrupted by our meeting. He'll moan and groan about some petty gripes; he'll claim he won't have time to do a thorough enough job of hand washing or that he had a certain trash can in mind to turn over and investigate. In the end, though, he'll come around and agree, pretending that he had something better to do although he really hadn't anything in mind in the first place. He just had to be his own petulant self.

Soon afterwards, Gabe came back. "Well, Phil, it's all set. Amanda was thrilled with the opportunity to observe humans in their native habitat. She relished the idea of turning the tables and acting as the observer rather than the observed. Al just nodded his head as if he had expected this message all along. Carrie spread her wings and flapped them vigorously. In fact, she stirred up quite a breeze. Only Sly sent out any negative vibes, mumbling something about needing to do a thorough hand washing and didn't anyone have any respect for thorough hygiene practices any more and besides he had a new trashcan to explore.

In the end, even he came around, though. Does he always make this much trouble, Phil?"

"Always and forever, Gabe. It's the same old, same old."

"You'd think that eternity would make some difference in the guy's attitude."

"Believe it or not, Gabe, it's my understanding that in some ways it has even though it's hard to see it."

"I'm off, Phil. Your next meeting is all set. You guys have an observation deck on Cloud Nine, overseeing the entire affair. In human time, you'll assemble promptly at 6:45 pm on your observation deck. At 7:00 pm, Adam will start his hunt for a mate of the moment. The whole affair should end before midnight is my best guess."

"Thanks, Gabe," I responded.

At 6:40 pm (human, pre-mortem time), in strode Amanda onto the observation deck of Cloud Nine. "Oh, I do look so forward to reversing roles and observing the humans with the same kind of detached, observant eye of judgment that these beings trained on us dogs in the old days. If you approve, Phil, I'll focus on the grooming habits of the male and female of the species. As a poodle, I have extensive experience in that department."

"As you wish, Amanda," Phil replied. "As for me, I lack your trained eye in that department."

Next Al slid in. "Phil, I've been thinking down there in my swamp that I'd like to focus on the predators in the crowd, the guys and gals who are out there to feed off the others. I want to see how as they sort of compete with each other for dominance."

"You're the one, Al." I shot back.

Then Carrie swooped down from above. She had soared even higher than Cloud Nine, and arrived promptly—to the exact second-- at 6:45 pm. "Phil, I'll observe the precise arrival and departure time of each human. How they deal with time says a great deal about them. Not always, but often enough, how the humans allocate their limited time discloses their values and emotions and personalities."

"I couldn't have said it better myself, Carrie. You're on." I beamed with joy. "This is gonna be easier than I thought," I reflected somewhat premature.

Then five minutes later in stumbled Sly, still sucking the booze from some discarded beer bottle that he must have gotten from some dumpster. Sly slowly shot each one of his colleagues a bleary eyed glance as they turned hostile, burning eyes on him. "Sorry, guys, I sort of got distracted, you know."

Amanda was outraged. "Sly, we don't want to listen to any excuses. We've chosen a job, a specialty, a focus. What's yours going to be?"

"Well, I, uh, you know hadn't quite thought of that," Sly mumbled as he let the beer can he was sucking the life out of slide from his mouth.

"Sly, your job will be to study the con games that are going on. You'll need to sit beside Al, whose specialty will be the dominance, predation, that's taking place. Dominance games and con games go hand in hand, so the two of you will have to work closely together," I determined. "Besides," I thought to myself, "Al will keep Sly in line. Sobering up almost instantaneously, Sly ambled over to a spot about a yard away from Al, all the while focusing on those sharp teeth that glistened from Al's half-opened mouth. "Hey, little buddy, come closer. I don't want to have to yell," Al bellowed. At this even I was a bit intimidated. I had never before realized how fear inspiring an alligator's roar could be. Visibly shaking, Sly nervously stepped a foot closer to Al, whose broad smile betrayed his amusement at the whole incident.

Now we were set to observe. I surveyed the park, where the event would occur. Adam had selected a park in mid-town, had secured the necessary permits, and circumvented the regulation about paying for an alcohol permit thirty days in advance. He had friends in the Parks Department. In fact, he had friend in every city and county office as well as a few in state and federal government. He regarded the small bribes he tendered his friends as just another petty business expense. He had also secured a local church hall in the event of adverse weather although his party had little to do with church. He had made a point of showering the church with donations. He made a point of being very democratic and equity-conscious in his bribes. He had even convinced himself that the bribes really weren't bribes at all but fundamentally payments for deluxe service. Adam had even calculated the timing precisely. Friday, October second, would have eleven hours and forty-nine minutes of daylight; the sun would set at 6: 07, allowing guests to come straight from or work. A few would even have time to freshen up and change wardrobes. It was an early fall day. Some of the trees had just begun to turn from the jungle green of the summer to the bright reds and oranges of autumn. He had torches and lights strung on the trees that lined the perimeter of freshly mowed lawn about the size of a football field. The trees still retained enough foliage to block out some of the view of the parking lot about two hundred yards from the lawn. Adam had bales of straw laid on either side of walkway from the parking lot to the field. Every other one had a pumpkin or large squash on top of it. There would be enough light to see and enough darkness to discuss private matters. I couldn't hold in my admiration. "I've really got to give, old Adam some credit. He knows how to throw a party." On the far side the field tables were loaded with serve yourself wine and beer although one table did offer a bartender who would serve mixed drinks. On the side opposite the drink tables, were tables laden with tailgate kind of food: barbequed chicken wings with two dozen types of sauces ranging from mild to spicy hot; grilled hamburgers; bratwursts; hot dogs; shish kabobs of chicken with peppers, onion, and zucchini; vegan alternatives to all of the meat listed beforehand; corn on the cob; coleslaw; garden salads; melon salads of watermelon, and cantaloupe topped with fresh strawberries; two different types of potato salad; pasta salads; buns and relishes and crescent rolls. In the far "end zone of the field, a jazz quartet played. On the field, twenty-five tables with four chairs apiece were spaced out at even intervals. I heard more than one reveler joke that they would go from table to table, zigzagging their way from one end zone to the other for their versions of a touchdown. "Yep," I had to confess, "this Adam guy knows how to throw a party. Sometimes, I could almost wish myself to be a pre-mortem human. But then I get to thinking about the real purpose of this bash, and I'm forever grateful that I am what I am."

Carrie kept her eye on the ones arriving early. It was 6:50 pm now. "Note how some of the early arrivals are glancing around nervously. One guy keeps looking at his watch as if he has something better to do. I'll wager that he doesn't. His watch addiction is probably a nervous habit. He follows rules almost slavishly, vainly trying to get ahead by coming off as more conscientious than everyone else. Another guy is almost blushing. He's keenly aware that the really important people haven't arrived yet and won't for some time. He's almost kicking himself for demonstrating that he has absolutely nothing better to do on a weekend night other than to attend this soiree and feel out-of-place. And then there's a young woman wringing her hands. I'll bet she's a new hire and wants to make a good impression. But none of the VIP's she hopes to impress have arrived yet, so she's wondering what impelled her to hustle home from work, shower, change, and rummage through her rather meager wardrobe to pick out her best dress. She had made arrangements to come with another young woman, also a new hire. Both seemed to be relying on the other for support. Perhaps she also sensed some danger in what's supposed to be a social gathering. We'll see."

"I think it's interesting that both the males and females of the species have evidently taken such care to select what they think are the best clothes for the occasion." The one man that Carrie observed as the first to arrive "is wearing a grey suit, with white shirt that has been starched almost to stiffness and a sky-blue tie with black wing-tip dress shoes. I'll bet that that this is his one and only suit. He must have stopped by the barbershop after work, for his precisely groomed short hair just barely long enough to comb over to the side sits in perfect aligment. He's sensing that he may have overdressed for the occasion and is already feeling out of place. The one male who entered next is trying a little too hard to come off as young and with it. He's sporting baggy black pants, the kind someone might wear to a gym, running shoes, and a an equally baggy shirt—not a sweat shirt but similar to one, with a V-neck so that his hairy chest hairs are available for all to see. He's got relatively long 3-4 inch hair that he has slicked back with just a touch of hair tonic. Still, I wonder where this Adam could be."

Out of habit, Al had buried himself in the cloud so that only his eyes and nostrils rose above the misty mass of water particles. He elevated his mouth only slightly before he spoke. "Don't worry, Amanda. Adam will make his entrance when about ninety per cent of his guests have arrived. He's got the instincts of a predator. He wants to have his pick of prey and that won't happen until the majority of the guests have arrived. VIP predators always come fashionably late."

"So, Al, just what or whom is this human predator pursuing?"

Sly couldn't restrain himself, "Oh, you know, the usual among humans: money and sex, sex and money."

"What about fame?" Amanda added.

"Nope, not this guy. He likes to lurk in the shadows and take advantage of easy kills. You know, this guy is sortta like me, I mean, in my foolish pre-mortem days," Sly concluded.

Al sunk lower in the mist so that he wouldn't bellow out what he was thinking. I observed him carefully. He was doing his best to preserve group harmony, and I had always assumed that alligators were loners. Anyway, I bet he wanted to put Sly in his place by adding that the old raccoon hadn't changed much post-mortem, but he held back, and I admired him for that. There would come a time to put Sly on notice, but not now. It was too early. Besides, Sly was right. Adam likes to hustle in the dark. You know, be a silent partner. Maybe that's another reason he came a bit late even though he and the senator had co-hosted the party. Adam had insisted that he remain a silent partner in the whole affair as befitted his status as lobbyist. I had looked up some information on Adam's activities before the party. Adam represented the interests of the RYJ Group. Although I've never been a student of Chinese, the RYJ is an acronym for *Rang Yangguang Jinlai*, Chinese for "Let the Sun Shine In." The Senator had made the Fifth Dimension's song "Aquarius, Let the Sunshine In" his campaign song and it clicked with the electorate. He promised a new age of Love, Peace, and Environmental Consciousness and his message resonated with the masses who had grown up with the legacy of the 60's celebrated by teachers, politicians, and Pop culture. Detractors insinuated that his theme of Love meant frequent sex with some of his staffers—female and male—that his theme of Peace meant the Press would keep their Peace and not investigate his sexual shenanigans, and, as for Environmental Consciousness, well Adam would take care of that. The RYJ group paid Adam handsomely (seven figures, but that figure didn't include a generous expense account) to represent their interests. And their interests consisted of landing US government contracts for solar panels. Now, I'm all in favor of environmental consciousness. I see my cousins struggling to cope with the environmental changes in Central Africa, and those changes mean loss of habitat and loss of life. Poachers, often from opposing armies of humans, have decimated some of the gorilla family groups, but the main changes relate to loss of habitat. So, I'm a big fan of environmental consciousness. But not when that consciousness simply white washes greater evils. So far, the solar panels constructed by RYJ don't do the job they are advertised to do. At best they can supply twelve percent of the energy required by the government offices. In fact, it takes more energy to produce these panels than any energy they can generate. It would take thirty years for the solar panels to break even energy-wise. But that doesn't make any difference to Adam and the Senator—right now these solar panels are generating lots of cash for them.

But it's time to return to observations. Adam had entered inconspicuously, quietly told the band to take a break, and slipped in a recording of The Fifth Dimension's "Aquarius, Let the Sunshine In" to be broadcast, but didn't turn it on until the spotlight shone on the Senator. Then he took the mike in the shadows and broadcast to the entire assemblage, the following message: "Who do we have to thank for this evening of pleasure under the stars? My friends, let me introduce to you a man who needs no introduction, Senator and, who knows, possibly our next president, Bobby Wainwright. Let's give it up for the man who will eliminate carbon emissions, save the rainforest, and save us from global catastrophe." The crowd applauded wildly, perhaps not just for all the reasons stated in the introduction to Senator Wainwright. By now more than a few revelers had had two or three drinks, a select few four or five. *In vino est veritas*, so they say, "In wine there's truth"; but some of those applauding most enthusiastically had little concern for truth as long as the booze kept flowing.

"Humans are a strange lot," Carrie observed. Some of them get so intoxicated that they resemble corpses when they pass out. I've seen some of these living corpses from my vantage point in the sky."

"Some of my cousins have claimed that they've feasted on drunk humans who fell overboard from their fishing boats and became the prey rather than the predator," Al added.

"All I know is that humans who've had a few more often than not leave tons of food around for me and my kind to feast upon, so their muddled minds aren't all bad."

"Look," I interjected. "Once the crowd stopped cheering Adam wrapped his arm around the Senator's shoulder and took him off to the shadows."

"Who's that fellow trailing Adam? Amanda asked.

"I think his name is Guy," I replied.

"Are you sure, Phil? I mean that would be like calling me Dog."

"Well, let's zoom in to their conversation."

"Adam, before you meet with the Senator, you might need this," the man whispered to Adam, extending his hand and handing over a fistful of something to Adam. Amanda observed that the mystery man sported a black turtleneck, with black pants and spit-shined black shoes.

"Whoa, whoa, whoa, now things are getting interesting" Sly exclaimed, rubbing his forepaws together. "The guy named Guy is handing over one of two things: a bag of drugs, probably cocaine, or a wad of bills, maybe fifties or hundreds."

"You're probably on target, Sly," I agreed. My best guess is that it's money. The Senator seems too savvy to be dealing with drugs in public. The money could cover a multitude of sins."

"I think you're spot on, Phil," Al added.

"There's something sinister about this Guy fellow, "Carrie intoned. "He walks in and out of the shadows."

"Let's wait and see what goes down between the Senator and Adam," I whispered even though there was no chance that either Adam or Senator Bobby could hear any of us. The two humans strolled off into the cover of the woods until the revelry of the crowd was only background noise.

"Senator, how'd you like my intro?" Adam asked opening the wad in his hand and then fanning out thirty or more one hundred dollar bills.

Forcing his eyes to turn away from the spread of money in front of him, the Senator dryly retorted, "The intro was spectacular, but I expected no less. Tell me, Adam, just how invested are your friends in my re-election campaign?"

"Heavily, can't you see?"

"Well, it's not going to be easy to be a walk in the park to make sure that your RYJ Company gets the contracts it wants. First of all, there's the matter of passing the energy bill with all of the incentives for alternative energy. Secondly, there's rumors that my likely opponent next fall is calling for amendments that would not only prioritize awarding contracts to American firms but would stipulate that only American firms—one hundred per cent American owned firms—could even bid on the contracts for the millions of solar panels the bill would call for. My re-election—and I might add—my support for RYJ is not a sure thing."

"So, what would make it a sure thing?" Adam asked, almost smirking.

"A million or two might take care of matters."

"It will be difficult to channel that much money to your coffers and still not make it obvious that the funds aren't coming from RYJ. We'll have to set up a number of ghost contributors."

Up on the cloud of the observation deck, Carrie cawed in disbelief. "What does Adam mean by 'ghost contributors'?"

"Carrie, my best guess is that Adam will set it up so that it looks as if hundreds, maybe more, individuals are donatin' cash to the Senator's campaign fund. That way, the Senator can not only bypass laws and regulations on who can give what to the Senator's treasure chest but also claim that he's got grass roots support from the ordinary people."

"I dunno, Carrie, but I bet he has it already figured out. Anyways, that's what I would do." Sly sat back smugly.

"Sly's got a point," I commented. "Let's see what happens."

The Senator and Adam talked a little while longer, shook hands, and then went their separate ways so that it wouldn't be obvious that the two had snuck off for a private rendezvous. They returned to the party scene from opposite ends of field, Adam re-entering from the area just behind the band. He had pre-planed this re-entry. First of all, by now almost half of the crowd had had a little too much to drink. The booze would render them benevolent and pre-disposed to making large donations. Over the next few days, he'd contact the donors and ask them if they'd like to contribute more—only they wouldn't be adding their own money. He'd be using slush funds provided by RYJ and by his friend Guy. He'd match their contribution, sometimes fivefold, as much as he could to the maximum allowed by campaign funds. "Who wouldn't be like to be known as a big spender—especially when they wouldn't even be spending their own money," Adam reasoned. This would be the start to his million –dollar bribe to the Senator. "A couple of thousand more, and I'll own the Senator," Adam whispered to no one but himself. Guy stood off by the edge of the woods, faintly smiling.

Once again, Adam asked the band to take a break and he played the fifth Dimension's "Aquarius, Let the Sunshine In." When the song had ended, Adam began his sales pitch. "Well, friends, first of all let's give a round of applause to the band and the cooks and the waiters and to all those who have made this evening one to remember." Here he paused to allow the almost perfunctory patter to end. Then he intoned again, this time more solemnly and earnestly. "Let's give special thanks to the one most responsible for tonight's gala festivities, Senator Bobby Wainwright." This time Adam led the cheering section, seconded by the raucous cheering, almost jeering of the man in black, Guy. On cue, the Senator strolled out from the opposite side of the field. "Now we all know that our friend and voice in the Senate Bobby Wainwright is up for re-election next year. If you support clean energy and a clean environment, then you need to show Bobby you care. Take out your checkbooks, dig into your wallets for whatever you can afford and let Bobby know that you care about the environment as much as he does. You can drop off your contributions by the bar and then have another round of drinks on your friend in the Senate, Bobby Wainwright."

"I guess our work for the evening is finished," Amanda said.

"I'd have to disagree, Amanda, but for a predator like Adam, the evening has just begun," Al commented and Phil nodded sadly.

THE WAY OF THE FLESH

"**A**L, WHAT DO YOU MEAN 'the night has just begun'? It's almost 10:30 human time."

"For Adam, only one goal has been achieved," Al observed, his huge mouth gaping open with all ninety-nine of his teeth glistening like stars.

"You've got it, Al. All that stuff going down with the Senator, that was like foreplay for old Adam. He was just flexing his muscles. Now it's time for the real action to begin." Sly could barely contain his enthusiasm as he rubbed his forepaws lustily. For these human types, it's all about power and sex, sex and power."

"Sex starts the long march towards death," Carrie declaimed. Didn't the Elizabethans believe that every sex act shortened one's life span by a day?"

"Let's just keep our focus on Adam and see what happens," Phil concluded.

Although the band would play on till eleven that night, a few people began leaving, thinning the crowd. From the shadows of the woods, Guy motioned with a slight turn of his head and shift of his eyes towards a lone woman. Adam knew perfectly well what his friend was signaling. Adam strolled over to the lonely figure who was searching the crowd. "May I help you? You seem to be looking for someone," Adam inquired in the most sincere voice he could muster.

"I'm looking for my friend, CeCe, Cecilia. She has short dark hair cut pixie style and was wearing a red, strapless dress."

"I think I saw her leaving about an hour ago in the arms of a young man," Adam replied, trying to come off as sympathetic for the plight of the abandoned woman.

"I should have known," the woman replied. "This wouldn't be the first time she's pulled this stunt."

"Who could abandon such pleasant company?" Adam asked. He seemed to be watching his words carefully. He wanted to sound sympathetic in an objective way.

"I'll bet that Adam is savvy enough not to sound as if he's trying to pick her up but only offering his help and consolation," Phil said.

"Yeah, this Adam guy is a smooth operator," Sly rejoined. "He knows from experience, I bet, how to play his game. He doesn't want to show his hand too early. He'll bluff by throwing out a smokescreen of kindness and benevolence. Yeah, he knows how to play this game."

"I'm appalled," Amanda replied. "Toying with emotions as if they are playing cards."

"I'm afraid, Amanda, that our Adam regards other humans just as means to an end," Phil concluded.

"But to what end?" Amanda stomped her right forepaw. "What can he hope to achieve?"

"It's all about ego," Al said. "About trying to be the biggest gator in the swamp. All predators are geared that way."

"Let's just listen. We can't intervene, just watch and then record." Phil put forefinger to his lips.

"Well, I do need a ride home now that CeCe is out of the picture."

"If you don't mind, I could give you a lift, but you'd have to wait until 11:30 or so. I'm co-hosting this event, so it wouldn't look good for me to slip away early."

"I'll wait, Mr. Adam Albright. I think I can trust you."

"You've got an advantage over me. You know my name, but I'm afraid I don't know yours. How did you know me?"

"Everyone knows who Adam Albright is. But I'm a new intern in your office, just started three days ago."

"How could I have missed you? My mind must have been lost in the storm of details swirling around getting this evening off the ground. I was tuning in to the weather channel every five minutes to make sure I didn't have to move the gala indoors. There's nothing more soothing than a night in October, the air cool and refreshing, the stars glistening in the dark sky, the leaves just beginning to turn."

"As an ardent environmentalist, I'm sure you love the outdoors. By the way my name is Francis. My friends call me Frannie."

"I hope I may be included in your list of friends, Frannie." Outwardly, Adam appeared to be a kindly father figure, his eyes moist with paternalistic care, his head tilted ever so delicately to the side. Inwardly, his mind was swirling with second thoughts.

"I'll bet that old Adam is trying to figure out how he can seduce her but still stay clear of any sexual harassment charges," Al observed. "On one hand, Frannie works in easy proximity; on the other hand, he's got to play his cards carefully and not show his hand too fast."

"You're right about that, bro," Sly observed. "I'll bet he takes it all slow, so he can claim that the two just fell in love. That is, until he tires of her."

Amanda stomped her right paw in protest.

Carrie just intoned, "It's the way of the flesh."

Phil added, "Est natura carnis, and that flesh is very weak, indeed."

That night, Adam exercised the most restraint he could muster to play the role of the benevolent father figure, shielding a young woman from the chicanery and duplicity of a hostile world. When the couple first entered the car, at first Adam said, nothing other than to ask where Frannie lived. Then he opened with his first lie. "Oh, just past Tenth Street. I'd have to pass by there on my way home. I've got to get up early for the Crusade Against Corruption rally at nine am tomorrow morning."

"Do you ever rest, Adam, I mean, Mr. Albright?" an impressed Frannie inquired.

"Oh, it keeps me busy. I mean there ought to be some purpose to our lives."

"OK, Phil, be straight with me," Sly asked from his vantage point in the clouds. "Is this Adam guy being straight or is he just lying through his pearly white teeth."

"He's equivocating, Sly. In some ways that's worse than lying. There is a rally against corruption tomorrow morning. Adam will make a brief appearance, leaving only when he's sure that plenty of people notice that he was there. But, as far as getting up early, well, that's a relative term. *Early* on a weekend means for Adam before noon. He's just trying to come off as some kind of secular saint."

"Yeah, I figured," Sly responded.

"This must be your address," Adam said. "I'll wait here until I'm sure you're safely inside. Or, if you wish, I'll escort you to the door."

"I'll be fine now, Mr. Albright. I can walk the thirty paces or so to my door, but I do appreciate the fact that you'll wait for me to be safe and secure. Thanks, so much. I guess I'll see you in the office on Monday. Thanks again. I just hope I haven't troubled you too much."

"Oh, no, not at all," Adam replied as he watched her make her way up the sidewalk and stairs to her second floor apartment. Then, talking to no one but himself, he said out loud. "I'll make sure that you pay for my services later."

"Man, this guy Adam should have born an alligator. He knows just how to camouflage himself. There've been more than one bird or beast that's mistaken me for just a drifting log in the swamp and then—" Al chose his words wisely. If he had been more specific, he knew he'd insult Sly. Many of Al's prey had consisted of unwary raccoons who had mistaken him for just driftwood.

"You know this Adam guy is just like some humans who want to come across as dog lovers in public. So they promenade around in public with their dogs, but the poor creatures live in filth and are fed only garbage. Then, when they tire of their pets, they euthanize them. I hope this Adam guy gets what's coming to him." By the time she had finished, Amanda was almost growling. "By the way, Phil, where's Adams's buddy, the one named Guy?"

"I lost track of him once he re-entered the woods. Maybe he figured that he could let Adam out on his own once he had set things up for him," I replied, rubbing my chin.

Carrie flapped her wings and then pronounced, "Evil to him who evil thinks."

"You're quoting from the motto of the order of the Garter, Carrie. I didn't know you were a student of history," I replied.

"All human history ends in a pile of bones," Carrie intoned.

Momentarily nonplussed, I didn't know how to respond, so I changed the subject. "Let's wait until the humans' Monday to see what happens," I declared. Al swished his powerful tail and swam away; Carrie took flight and soared through the high heavens; Sly ambled away; and Amanda just sat and waited until the others had left. "Phil, I guess Carrie was right about human history and all, but what about the spirit?"

"That's what we have to deal with, Amanda," I reflected. See you human time next Monday morning at nine am."

"Good-bye, Phil. Thanks."

"I'm just doing my job, Amanda." I responded. "I just never knew that eternity would involve so much work and so many painful thoughts."

When all of my colleagues had left and gone their separate ways, I felt so terribly alone. But just when I started to feel sorry for myself, Gabe burst in faster than a lightening bolt. "I've got orders, Phil. You're to report to heaven ASAP for a little R & R." Then off he flew, leaving me nothing better to do than to be transported to bliss. You see, we animals lived our lives on earth and followed natural law, and Nature can be very cruel, you know. Just ask Al. By exercising free will and accepting the grace freely given them, humans can win a spot in heaven in either heaven or hell right after they're post-mortem. With us animals, it's different. We get free will and the blessings of grace, post-mortem and exist in a kind of purgatorial state along with humans who sortta did the right things most of the time but not always. We're on a level plain with them in this in-between state although for the most part we maintain a safe distance from each other. Anyway, I needed my taste of total bliss as an incentive to keep going.

And promptly at 8:50 am on Monday morning in human time, I occupied my vantage point on our cloud and waited the entry of my colleagues. Amanda soon followed, as did Al and Carrie. Sly stumbled in, reeking of decaying pizza fragments and stale beer. "Oh, man, I that dumpster by the frat house was too much. You know, I didn't know that anybody still ate anchovy pizza. Yu learn something new every day." I guess Sly had fallen into his version of heaven.

"Let's see what Adam is up to," I advised.

"I'll bet he's gonna be Mr. Smooth operator," Al forecast. "He's gonna follow up on his role as protector and environmental crusader to whitewash his real intentions."

"I could just shake that Frannie girl," Amanda exclaimed. "She's wearing her best outfit, a kind of body suit all made with completely recycled materials, of course. It's all in different shades of green but doesn't do much to camouflage her figure. She even showed up for work half an hour early. I've been watching her."

"Humans are their own worst enemies," Carrie intoned.

"Let's be quiet and just observe," I advised. And so they did. "On most Mondays the book says that Adam arrives about twenty minutes late. Let's see what he does this time."

Adam strolled in two minutes before nine, checked in with his secretary Connie to see when his first appointment was. With Connie, Adam was all business even though she was considered quite attractive, at least by human standards. "Any appointments, Connie?" he asked.

"You've got a three o'clock meeting with the Senator over at his campaign headquarters. That's all."

"Maybe we've been too harsh on Adam," Amanda reflected. "He acts very professionally with his secretary."

"Well, there's history there. It's recorded in the book here." I responded. "You see, when Connie first started working for Adam, she did so because the hours were somewhat flexible and she still got medical benefits. Adam convinced himself that she wanted the job because she wanted him. No way. On the first day of work, he pressed her shoulder a little too intimately and asked her out to lunch. 'I treat all my employees to lunch on their first day,' Adam explained. Connie sensed his real motives but decided she had to accept the invitation. In a dimly lit corner of a local restaurant, Adam made his move, somewhat clumsily. After they had ordered their food, he pressed Connie's hand a little too intimately. Connie reacted swiftly and definitively, 'So, do you flirt with your male employees, too. You swing both ways, Adam? You do that again and I'll slap you with a sexual harassment suit so fast your head would spin. And my husband is a cop He knows how to use his 9mm." The last thing Adam needed at that moment was the negative publicity from a sexual harassment suit, so he sulked away with his tail between his legs, so to speak, and sought out other less combative prey. If he tried to fire her, he knew she would retaliate and, besides, he thought, she had two young children and he didn't want that kind of baggage."

"Oh, I was hoping Adam had some good in him," Amanda sighed.

"I suppose he does," I replied. "But it's hard to find."

"He's got the instincts of a predator. I should know," Al stated matter-of-factly. You see when a predator figures out that he might get wounded in an attack he or she backs off, having done sortta a risk analysis of the situation."

"Let's see what the dude does next," Sly added, He had even taken some time to wash his hands and the rest of his reeking body.

Adam went inside his private office and drummed his fingers on his cherry wood desk for a few minutes and then left and walked to the rear of the office space, where he knew he'd find Frannie. "You look stunning," he said and then checked himself. I figured he'd figure that he had come across a little too obviously. So, he tried to regain lost ground. "I'll bet that your suit is made of completely recycled material, Frannie. I wish the rest of my staff would be environmentally conscious as you are."

"Well, Mr. Albright—Adam—you know what they say, 'It's not enough to talk the talk, you've got to walk the walk.'"

"Right you are, Frannie. How do you like your job?"

"It's my dream job," Mr. Albright.

"Well, how about we talk things over at lunch? I know a nice quiet place just a five minute walk from here."

"That would be great. Thanks, Mr. Albright."

"Think nothing of it, Frannie. I do that for all of my new employees. I like to get to know them. See what makes them tick. We'll walk down about 12:30."

"Fine, see you at 12:30."

Around noontime, Connie asked Frannie if she'd like to join her and two or three others who worked in the office for lunch. "We laugh and joke, then get ready for the afternoon grind," Connie explained.

"Thank you very much," Frannie replied, "but I already have lunch plans."

"Would those plans include Mr. Albright?" Connie asked, fixing her sky blue eyes straight at the young intern.

"Well, yes," Frannie stumbled through her words. "I thought it was customary."

"Well, I guess you're right there, Frannie." And then after a long pause, Connie added, "But some customs are more honored in the breach rather than in the observance. Well, enjoy your time with the boss, but be careful."

"Oh, I'm always careful. Some people claim that that's one of my main faults."

Frannie turned and left. She still had half an hour before her lunch date with Mr. Albright. "What could Connie mean with that warning to be careful?" she mumbled out loud in the almost deserted office.

Promptly at 12:30, Adam Albright emerged from his private office. "Well, Frannie, shall we go?" he invited, taking her hand. "You'll love this place. Although you can order almost anything you want, their specialty is French cuisine. You'll love it."

The intern balked a little bit, still unnerved somewhat by Connie's warning, but she soon abandoned any doubts when they walked hand in hand the two sort blocks to the restaurant in the crisp autumn air.

"If all goes well with our solar panel projects, the air will be even purer than it is today: no more coal smoke belching from outdated furnaces, just the sun's rays invigorating the world—with a little help from modern technology. Just envision a green new world."

"Yes, that will be a paradise on earth," Frannie commented.

The couple soon reached their destination, a restaurant named *La Poule Francais.* It was tucked away in a small alcove with black iron railings and a brick façade. "All that brick," Adam explained, "came from demolished buildings. We like to recycle everything."

"Of course," Frannie responded as Adam opened the door for her.

"As I said, you are free to order as you wish, but, if you prefer, you may simply, feast on the luncheon menu I have pre-selected—to save time. We do, alas, have to return to work. The specialty of the house, actually my specialty, consists of three small but infinitely delicious dishes: Escargot in butter sauce, French Onion Soup, and then Coq au Vin. We can decide on dessert later."

Dazzled from the glistening lights of the huge chandelier that hung from above, Frannie just quickly responded, "Oh, I'm sure that your specialty will suit me well."

"Come, I've already made arrangements with the maître d'. We'll feast on the second floor. To compensate for the lack of floor space, the restaurant featured three floors, all connected by a circular stairwell sitting in the center. The maître d' escorted the couple to the second floor and then with a flourish of his arm signaled them to sit in a far corner, remote enough to block any views by curious onlookers.

"Hey, Phil, that maître d' fellow looks a lot like Guy, you know the one we saw at the park last Friday," Sly burst out.

Amanda crouched low, as if preparing to spring on some unwary rabbit, and fixed her gaze on the black-clad man, "Sly's right, Phil. What's going on here?"

"This looks like a team effort from known predators, circling some careless prey. But what I want to know is what's in it for Guy?" Al questioned.

"Let's see what happens next," Phil determined.

The couple engaged in a flurry of small talk: what got you interested in the green movement, where did you go to school, what are your plans for the future, etc. When the couple had finished their soup and were waiting for the Coq au Vin to be served, Adam pressed Frannie's hand ever so lightly and said in the sincerest tone he could muster, "Thanks for this afternoon, Frannie. It means so much to me to know how invested you are in what could become our joint mission."

"Oh, no, Adam—it is all right if I call you Adam? —it's I who should thank you."

As two finished their meal, Adam inconspicuously wrapped his arm around Frannie's waist and then promptly removed it when they exited onto the bustling street. Guy looked at them and just smirked.

MONEY TALKS

A s the couple entered the office, both were scrupulously all business, Adam speaking about a new grass roots approach that he had been developing and Frannie listening attentively and hoping that she, too, could play a role. Connie just turned her head away, for she realized that was sending out an eye-roll that she couldn't deny. After a formal farewell, Adam opened the door to his office and reflected that he had slightly more than an hour. On his desk, Connie had laid a message from the Senator: "Meet at the park just behind where the band played last Friday night."

"So, ole Senator Bobby Wainwright wants some privacy. Well, prying eyes and ears, human and electronic, are everywhere. I guess the Senator has been through this before after seventeen years in office. I wonder when his pension kicks in?" A few taps on they keyboard revealed that ole Bobby boy had already qualified for a pension because of his age and years of service. "Well, the old guy has it made." Adam grinned. "Now the question is how much will he get? He can't get more than eighty per cent of his salary, but, hell, after he retires from Congress, he can spend a little time in some dark hole doing who-knows-what and then officially or unofficially lobby. He'll be rolling in dough."

"Yep, that's how it works," observed Al. "Those that make the rules make the money as well. The first principle of governance is that money talks."

"But, when they die, they all stink the same, rich or poor, powerful or helpless," added Carrie.

"This just isn't right," objected Amanda.

"So, how do you get to be a senator?" asked Sly.

"Let's see what kind of scheme Adam comes up with," concluded Phil. "So far everything seems to be going his way."

"Yeah, well that's what a bottomless pit of money will do for ya," commented Sly. "It takes money to make money, so I've heard the humans say. And this RYJ Company seems to have lots of cash to throw around."

"Aren't there campaign finance laws, though?" wondered Amanda.

"Yeah, there are, but Adam's job is figure out ways to get around these legal impediments," snapped Al. "Look how he's getting around the sexual harassment laws. If he and Frannie break up—which they'll do sooner or later—he'll claim that the two of them fell in love or some such nonsense but then both realized that the relationship had to end tragically—as if the two of them are Romeo and Juliet."

"You seem to know a lot about these affairs, Al," Amanda shot back.

"Well, there's a lot of down time in the swamp," he retorted.

"Phil, aren't there laws against a boss having an affair with a subordinate, especially an intern twenty years younger that he—or she—is?" Amanda asked.

"Well, I've seen cases like this before. If anybody calls attention to the alleged affair, the first thing the predator will do is to deny anything took place. He'll be careful to avoid any PDA's; he'll always pay cash for meals and hotel rooms; he'll use assumed names. Did you see how Adam composed his face? Right before he entered the office door, he had the leer of an old lecher and the gait of a satyr. After he opened the door, he re-sculptured himself to come off as just a grandfatherly mentor, ushering in a novice to the world of business. I'm sure he's got even more tricks up his expensive Italian suit sleeves than the ones I've mentioned. Let's tune in to see what he's up to next.

Adam devoted the next few minute to reviewing his notes. He had planned the meeting with the Senator scrupulously. At 2:45 he exited his private office, told Connie he would be out for the afternoon. Connie nodded as if she had heard all of this before. He parked his car a five -minute walk away from the rendezvous point. Without being obvious, he surveyed the area as if he were just a bored executive taking in Nature.

"I've got to give old Adam credit," Sly exclaimed. "The guy knows how to play the game. He looks bored and blasé even while his heart must be pumping and the adrenaline's kicking in. Yeah, and the old Senator ain't no slouch, either. He had picked out a place where there was only one bench. He sat on one end and Adam meandered his way over to the other end. These guys are old pros."

"Keep a lid on it, Sly," Amanda whispered. "I want to hear every word they say."

"You know there are campaign laws against accepting money from foreign companies. I want no part of violating those laws. Hell, I wrote some of them myself." The Senator spoke as if he were making a general statement to some unseen audience."

"I know one All-American company that would like to see Senator Wainwright win first the primary, as he has already done, and then the general election."

"I like All-American companies, so do my constituents. So, what makes a company All-American?"

"Well, for one, all of the workers are American citizens, several are veterans. They have to show proof of citizenship and the veterans, who get preferential treatment in hiring and promotion, have to show their Honorable Discharge and DD214."

"Now, you've got me interested. Let's take a little walk in the woods, shall we?" The Senator looked around as if he were trying to determine the most scenic path. Adam rose and the two walked side-by-side except in those places where the path narrowed.

"Man, I like the Senator's style," Sly burst out. "He chose a place and a time where there'd likely be no crowd, no ears to hear what the two are cookin' up and no eyes to see them together. If anybody questions what went on, each one of the two can say they just went for a little relaxing stroll. I'll bet that not even electronic ears can hear what they're talkin' about."

"No, Sly, but we can," Phil broke in. "Let's be still so we can drink in all that they're saying,"

"Yes, please, Sly, for once be quiet and listen," Amanda almost barked back.

"Yeah, yeah, yeah, all right," Sly replied. Al just glared menacingly.

"So, what's the name of this company, Adam?" inquired the Senator.

"Well, serendipity strikes in. You'll recognize the name: it echoes your campaign theme, 'Let the Sun Shine In.' It's the perfect name for a company that manufactures solar energy panels."

"How many employees are there?"

"Fifty-two, Senator, and thirteen of them are veterans."

"I haven't heard of many American companies that make solar energy panels. I thought that almost all of the panels came from China."

"It's true that many of the parts do come from China, but all of the assembly is done stateside, and the panels are shipped out with 'Assembled in America by American Workers' stamped prominently on each and every box. On a technicality, we can't claim 'Made in America,' you know how these things roll."

"What if this company you speak of made the maximum contribution to my campaign?"

"Not a supercilious hair would be raised, Senator."

"Still, the maximum contribution such a company would make would be peanuts. I hope you've got a little more time to make this walk through the woods entertaining."

"I think I've got the support of some labor unions. For sure, I've got the Teachers' Union on board for major contributions to a Super PAC."

'Well Adam, it looks as if you've got your work cut out for you. I need cash, not nebulous promises of 'I think's.'"

"Oh, I've got cash, Senator. In fact, I'm swimming in a sea of cash, only we're going to use it in a different way. You still need the Super PAC to fund TV ads, but the wave of the future lies in social media."

"Note that the campaign laws state that uncompensated individuals may use the internet without restriction to express their political views. Hell, there isn't even a limitation on uncompensated blogging."

"So, just how do you get a network of unpaid workers to campaign for my re-election?" The Senator seemed dubious.

"That's where the cash comes in. We offer cash 'expressions of gratitude' to those who take on your campaign altruistically. We slip them the money in a setting like this. They'll soon get the message that the more they promote you the more 'expressions of gratitude' they'll get."

"How will you start this? Adam, it looks as if you are setting up the groundwork for a kind of pyramid scheme, but getting those first bloggers or whatever won't be easy."

"Oh, I've got help there." Out of the woods stepped Guy, all dressed in black, his camouflage apparel. "Senator, you may have seen Guy at your rally last Friday although if you've saw him, you probably wouldn't remember him. He makes it his business to be utterly inconspicuous. Guy has been attending Environmental rallies and sounding out potential bloggers, especially ones who both passionate about solar energy and in need of money. He offers no money up front, but he already has seven bloggers on the payroll, ones who have accepted money to defer their expenses, of course."

"And, I suppose we can expect those seven to recruit another seven or more to the cause?"

"Precisely, Senator."

"And all are paid in cash, small bills, of course."

"That goes without saying."

"And so where does this ocean of cash come from?"

"You don't need to know that. Let's just say I have contacts."

"So, if any nosey reporters stick their noses in, there's no connection to me?"

"Absolutely none."

"I'll disavow any ties to you if we're caught and maintain that you took advantage of my friendship."

"I wouldn't have it any other way."

"Then, what's in it for you?"

"Let's just say, Senator, that you and I share certain friends in the solar energy field. That's all you need to know." Of course, the Let the Sun Shine In company as an American firm employing veterans at a rate over twenty-five per cent of its work force should get favorable treatment in the awarding of government contracts for the solar panels."

"Of course, that only makes sense—and good politics."

Even in the afternoon sun, Guy's black outfit blended in with the shadows of the dark woods. With a slight jerk of his head, Adam motioned him to join in the conversation "Don't be alarmed, Senator. Guy has been circling us all the time, making sure that no one else would accidentally or purposefully overhear our conversation. He plays a vital role." He extended his hand for the Senator to shake. His grip seized the Senator's hand as if he wasn't just shaking hands; Guy was squeezing the hand in a vise grip.

Up on the cloud, Al commented, "Guy has something about him that strikes me as unnatural. I've seen my share of vicious predators—I was among them—but this Guy lurks on the fringes of reality. We need to keep our eyes out for him."

When Guy released the Senator's hand, Guy took out a wad of cash and fanned it front of the astonished Senator, who blurted out, "How much are you carrying?"

"Oh, Senator, it's not as much as you think. It's all five- dollar bills. What you saw amounted to only two hundred dollars, but flashing forty greenbacks makes an impression. Environmental activists aren't paid that much, so that when a make a kind of peacock display of cash I get their attention. When I tell them that I'm just covering their expenses and that all I want to do is to compensate them for their blogs extolling the virtues of solar energy, they jump at the chance. It all sortta gives a new meaning to 'Going Green.' Company. By then they're so enmeshed in our scheme and so dependent on our money that they'll write anything we want them to. So, I give them campaign literature from the Senator's own office that details his commitment to solar energy and to American owned, veteran-friendly businesses like Let the Sunshine In. Then I offer them bonuses to recruit other bloggers."

"So, it's a pyramid scheme," the Senator remarked. "Only better than the typical ones. I'll bet that they've convinced themselves that their motives are utterly altruistic, that the apostles of environmentalism deserve some recompense and all the while they're doing our bidding." Then the Senator paused a bit as if he were thinking better of the whole matter. "But I don't want my name tied directly to any of this."

"Oh, Senator, don't worry. Your name is completely out of this. I employ only trusted, long-term agents using aliases to distribute the cash. The bloggers and other social networking writers we employ never see the faces of our agents, only the great mountains of cash in front of them. These operatives won't even realize that they're being paid to advance your cause until they're completely mired in the quicksand of our little enterprise. If they would do anything as unlikely as protest it all, they'll be sucked under by the cash they've accepted."

"Yeah, Sly observed from his perch above, "As I was sayin', money talks." Amanda shot Sly a glance that blazed like a thunderbolt of scorn. Al sunk deeper into the depths of the cloud. Carrie cawed, "It's the rot of the flesh." And flew off. As for me, I just shook my head and wondered what role I should play next. Obviously, my initial appearance to Adam hadn't had any effect at all. He just dismissed it as a bad dream, an early morning bout of miasma. And then there's Frannie. How will Adam corrupt her?

As for the Senator, when he returned from his meeting with Adam, he dialed his financial advisor and told him to invest a cool million in some obscure firm named Let the Sun Shine In.

SIREN SONGS OF SEDUCTION

AFTER MY COLLEAGUES HAD LEFT, I decided to keep an eye on Adam. In the woods, the Senator left first. Then, headed in opposite direction, Guy took off five minutes later. Adam lingered a bit as if he planned to return to his office after everyone else had headed home. He expended some nervous energy by walking the circumference of the park, a little more than three miles and then dallying for a while in front of a fountain where dryads and satyrs were sculpted into an eternal chase. A little after five pm, he headed back to his car and then drove to the office.

The drive home gave Adam time to think. I really wish he'd re-think what he's up to. Me and my whole species have suffered enough. We don't need some humans discrediting the whole environmental issues just because they want to drive faster cars, eat more expensive meals, snort more cocaine, and have sex with more partners, whom they sooner or later tire of and then toss aside. Yep, it's time for another apparition, something that might shake old Adam to the bones. But what kind of apparition? As I said, the first one didn't go so well. He just laughed it off, like some kind of Halloween prank. I don't know. I guess I'll have to talk it over with my crew. But we won't meet for a day or two or three in human time. I guess I'll just keep watch over Adam and mull things over.

Let's take a little look at what thoughts Adam is churning in his mind while he thinks he's safe in the confines of his car. A lot of humans talk out loud when they're in their cars. They make conversation with themselves even while they're muttering about some mistake the driver in front of them made.

"I couldn't have planned it any better," Adam said to no one other than himself. "I've got the Senator in my pocket, and Guy's agents will make sure he stays there. The cash from RYJ will just keep rollin' in. We've set things in motion so that the Senator will come off as a leader with grassroots support. By the time we're finished we'll have thirty bloggers with hundreds, maybe thousands of readers singing the praise of the Senator from the Age of Aquarius, a man of the people and for the people and, of course, the planet. Hell, in a couple of weeks, we may even be able to coast a little and just let Fate take its course. Now that I've got my hands on the old Senator's wallet, I need to figure out how to get my hands down young Frannie's pants." Just then I heard high-pitched, discordant screeching noises. Adam drove his foot to the floor jamming on the brake pedal. "Damn it, why the hell can't people learn to drive?" Adam cursed. From my perspective, up above, the other driver wasn't at fault. Adam had gotten so caught up in his own self-congratulatory delusions that he had lost sight of the car in front of him. But in his own mind, at least, Adam could do no wrong. So, he blared on the horn. A few other drivers, frustrated by rush hour traffic, joined in the cacophony of blaring car horns. I guess doing so made them feel better—sort of like when I get to chest thumping just for the sake of chest thumping. Anyway, the rest of the drive to the office was anti-climactic.

Adam slammed his car door shut as he strode back to the office. "Good, the lights are all out, everyone's gone home or wherever the hell they go after work, and I've got the whole space to myself. He jammed his key into the lock and slammed the office door for good measure, and headed to the comforting solitude of his private office. He eased himself down into his leather upholstered chair, took out a glass, and poured himself out a double Scotch from the bottle of single malt He regaled himself with the pleasure of the warm whisky easing its way down his gullet. At this point I could almost sympathize with Adam. Back in my earthly days, I shared a cool Budweiser with my trainer, and nothing could beat the joy of that cool brew going down. But a lot of humans don't know when to stop. If one is good, they reason, two or three or six or seven would be better, so they drown themselves in booze. And this is what Adam did. At least, the guy kept to his chair and didn't try to drive home. He'd pass out and then snap out of it and five or six hours later, drive home, shower, and change and be back at work the next morning. So, he drowned himself in boozy thoughts of how he'd seduce Frannie. At first, he was careful, even rational in a sinister kind of way. "I've got to go slow. I'll let a few days pass and then I'll make an excuse to wend my way over to her desk and compliment her on her work and ask if there was anything I could do to make her happy in her new position. No, I'd better cut out that last line. By asking if there was anything I could do to make her happier, she might sense that that was a come-on line. I gotta drop that. Then maybe a little later, next week, I'll call her into my office to confer. That will make her feel important and valued. Everyone likes that. I'll seek out her advice on some trivial matter but make it sound all-important. Yeah, we're developing that television spot from the Super-PAC money we got. I'll run a script of that thirty -second ad for her and ask her what she thinks of it. Then I'll gradually ask her to my office more and more and, who knows, we might even have to work overtime into the dark of the evening. Have a few drinks. Yeah, that'll do it." After Adams's fourth drink, his thoughts became incoherent and he probably lost himself in boozy dreams of sleeping with Frannie.

I relayed all of these observations to my colleagues to seek out their advice. I knew an apparition was in order. I just didn't know how to pull one off that would have any effect.

Al voiced the first opinion at our small convocation of five. "You know, I got to hand it to that guy Adam. He knows how to mask his movements, keep his intentions hid, you know like being submerged in the swamp. He's a clever predator who will wait for his opportunity and then snatch it in his jaws. With that in mind, Phil, I propose that we bring him out in the open, call his bluff, and let him know that we know what's going on. This is no time for subtlety. This time for action."

"Al's right," Amanda seconded. "Adam gets his way because no one calls him out. I think that folks don't point out the evil in Adam because they don't want to admit to the evil in themselves. Besides, Adam is crafty. He'll seduce people with money, win them over with boozy friendships, and then strike. We must call him out—no question about that."

Sly had been shifting about guiltily. He must have seen a lot of himself in Adam and had been searching for a way to deflect the conversation away to a different consideration. "You know, we need to act like a pack in concert. Back in my pre-mortem days, I'd seek out my buddies to pull off my escapades. Two or three of us would work as a team to get that trash can pulled down or to pop open a lid or a door. We got to act as a team."

"For once, I agree with Sly. He's got a point. What's the sense of the five of us working to observe Adam if we also don't work as a team to act in his best interests—even if he may not see it that way?" Amanda stomped down with her right forepaw to stress her point.

I rubbed my chin maybe a little too vigorously. "You guys make a lot of sense. We need to appear together, act in concert, to warn Adam to mend his ways. It's our only chance. Maybe he can shrug off just one of us, but he'll have a harder time trying to ignore the five of us. What do you think, Carrie? You haven't said anything yet." I knew that Carrie was listening—she always listened—and that she had a unique perspective on things.

Carrie flapped her wings and took off for a brief flight in the heavens. Then she settled down and pronounced her verdict. "Adam lives in the pre-mortem realm of the flesh too much so. He requires a memento mori or at the very least a vision of himself in a few sort years—a sad, lonely ageing crippled satyr, hobbling around looking for prey nowhere to be found."

Usually, Carrie spoke in a few monosyllables. For her, this was a lengthy speech. Amanda seconded Carrie's proposal, as did Al, who knew from experience that flesh decays, rots, and stinks. Sly tacitly went along with the proposal, giving it a paw's up.

"Then the general outline of our apparition is set," I concluded. "The five of us will all appear in one vision, startle Adam, and give him a grim vision of himself in a few years. It may not work—Adam has had over forty years to become the man he is—and we may have only forty seconds, but at least we've got a plan."

Meanwhile Adam was executing his strategy. He ignored Frannie for three days. So successfully was this approach that she wondered what she had done wrong. In her mind she retraced every single minute at work, desperately trying to detect a flaw that wasn't there. Finally on the fourth day, Adam strolled over to her desk. She had been working on revisions to the television spot for the Senator. Adam had let her know of the PAC money but kept his cash payments to bloggers a secret. Even his secretary Connie, who really ran the office and was far more aware of specific details than was Adam, didn't know about the network of paid-in-cash operatives. Frannie didn't know what to expect but suspected the worst. The worst was coming though not in the manner she had envisioned. Then breaking from his diffidence, Adam broke out in a friendly smile. "I hear you've been doing great work on the Senator's TV spot. Give me your honest assessment."

At this comment, Frannie beamed. "The opening with the theme song of 'Aquarius, Let the Sunshine In,' is visually spectacular with the flood of rainbow colors and the tempo of the music putting the audience in an upbeat mode, ready for the good things to come. And those good things do come. The message about saving the planet comes out loud and clear as the audience catches sight of a globe spinning wildly out of control. Then Senator Wainwright stops the globe and yells out 'Enough'—It's time we repair all the damage to the only world we know. Vote for me in the general election. Show that you care. If you can, donate to my campaign. Every little bit helps. If we show that we care, we can win this one for ourselves for our children, for our children's children, and for the planet. Then we'll truly see the dawning of a new age as we save the Earth and save ourselves.' Frannie finished her summary, perhaps to impress her boss with just how immersed in the project she was. But then she added her own insights. "All of that is great. There's just one problem. In the background, the crowd that follows the Senator is too old, too white, and too ordinary. We need to add a splash of color to that crowd: black people, brown people, young and old, well dressed and barely dressed. We need to show that the Senator attracts all stakeholders."

"Brilliant, Frannie," Adam replied earnestly. "My thoughts exactly. Come to my office at 11:30. We'll work out the details of a new shoot of a new crowd, one more universal in scope. Then we'll celebrate with a lunch at my favorite place." Then he did a quick about face and returned to his office to gloat.

When Adam rested securely in his private lair, Connie walked over to Frannie and said matter of factly: "You know, Adam can be a great guy to work for. He pays great, gives trusted employees a lot of consideration when they're dealing with medical or family issues, the benefits are good—"

"You're going to throw in *a but*, Connie, aren't you?"

"You read my mind, girl," Then Connie turned her face to the side as if thinking of issues long since past or word choices designed to warn but only in an oblique way. 'You don't have to go along with everything Adam says or implies. You're smart, educated, young, and a looker. Make your own decisions and do right for you. In the long run, the boss will respect you for that."

"That's easy for you to say, Connie. You've been here like forever. I don't even have the guarantee of a full-time job. I know you're looking out for me, but I can make my own decisions." Now Frannie turned away brusquely and headed to her desk where she took a moment to review the menu for her lunch date.

Connie just shook her head and muttered so that no one except me and my confederates could hear: "Damn, that Frannie girl reminds me of my seventh grade daughter sometimes. If I say anything else, she'll brush me off and tell me to mind my own business."

The lunch date went even better than Adam had hoped. Frannie asserted herself in a mild way by ordering her own lunch—although she didn't offer to split the bill. But she didn't order the most expensive dish on the menu, either, so I could she made a declaration of independence.

Her small gesture evoked praise from her boss. "Good, Frannie, you're starting to assert yourself. I admire that quality, especially in a woman. I've been turning over some ideas in my head about those revisions in the TV spot. I just can't get a fix of the right mix of people to cast in the crowd scene. Which ones do we present up close and which ones just form part of the crowd. I'm afraid we're bound to offend one group while we feature another. And I wonder who we're leaving out. Every revision calls for another revision and another and another. The more we try to be inclusive, the more we come off as exclusive." Here

Adam paused and sipped his glass of wine while his blazing eyes bored straight through Frannie's. He got the desired result. "Would you be able to work through this dilemma, say on Friday after everyone else has left and we won't be distracted?"

"Of course, Adam." She smirked as if she knew this question was coming.

"All right, then, Friday it is." And Adam raised his glass as if for a toast. Frannie joined him.

"Man, I admire the old guy's style, "Sly commented. "He's an old pro at this game."

"Don't be too sure, Sly," Al interjected. We'll see how this plays out."

"Well, we've got our planning to do—about the apparition." Amanda insisted.

Still a little wounded by the failure of my solo attempt at converting Adam from the error of his ways, I blurted out. "What are our plans? How will the five of us appear?"

Carrie broke the silence. I'll swoop down. We'll use Adam's full-length mirror—the one he checks himself with before he goes out. I'll swoop down."

"And I'll surface from bottom of the mirror from a brackish-looking pool," All added.

"I'll be howling like a coyote from the right side." Amanda stuck her best coyote pose, upraising her head and howling to the stars.

"And me, I'll come in from the left subbing my hands in satanic glee, grinning all the while," Sly volunteered.

"Well, Phil, you've got to be the man in the middle, issuing a solemn warning to Adam," Al concluded.

"Well, Adam was right about one thing: it's tough to figure out the right mix when so many voices are present," Phil concluded. "I guess it can't be much worse than the first one I tried to pull off solo."

Despite their best efforts, Adam was unimpressed. Phil intoned a simple message with a booming voice and hostile glare. With his forefinger raised, he exclaimed. "Sooner than you think this will be you." Then the image of the five faded to be replaced with a clip of a pot-bellied satyr, whose face looked a lot like Adam's, hobbling around with his wrinkles rippling in the twilight, chasing nubile dryads who mocked his feeble efforts to snatch them. Adam looked at the images with disdain. "This is Looney Tunes only not as funny. That's not me and never will be! I've got to give up that afternoon snort at least for a little while."

THE SEDUCER SEDUCED

HIGH UP IN THE CLOUDS, Amanda slunk in to the observation desk, her head hanging low and her tail dragging along behind. She dutifully sat down and awaited my arrival. Usually, I'm the first one there so that I can greet all of my colleagues as they enter, for the most part one by one. But not this time. This time I sensed that we had failed and I dreaded debriefing the previous night's proceedings. "I guess we bombed," muttered Amanda. She was usually in such an upbeat mood that I feared I had failed her, too. I walked in on all fours. No chest thumping this time.

But I had to change the mood. Not that I'd lie or anything, but I owed it Amanda to try to swing her around to her usual perkiness. "Well, Amanda, I guess our little apparition thing didn't go as we had expected. This Adam fellow seems impervious to our best efforts, but we're not finished yet. We've got to celebrate the small victories. At least, we got him to lay off the cocaine for a few days. Still, by Saturday night he'll probably be back to his afternoon habit of snorting, sort of his version of high tea."

"Hey, Phil, I overheard your joke as I was making my way in. I like that—'his version of high tea.' I might even use that when the right time comes around." Al was all smiles. "You know I got to thinking about our little apparition fiasco. It wasn't all bad. As Phil said, at least we weaned Adam away from his coke habit for a little while. Our timing was bad, that's all. To persuade someone, you got to appeal to reason, emotion, and ethics—only in this case we can forego ethics, as Adam hasn't evolved enough to have many ethical concerns other than winning. But timing is everything. We're gonna have to be patient. You know, sit in the swamp for a little while and wait until Adam screws up. Then maybe he'll listen to what we have to offer. As it stands right now, everything is going his way. Like a lot of guys, he suffers from the Peter Pan syndrome. He thinks he's an eternal frat boy on an endless party kick. It's all one big joke. He's got to experience that the joke is on him first. Then, maybe, he'll be open to change."

"You're my man, Al," Sly bellowed. "I couldn't have said it better myself. You got to know when to strike and when to hold back to pull off any caper. Back in the old, earthly days, me and my crew would hole up until the humans were fast asleep. Only when we were positive that they were out in la-la land, dreaming of who-knows-what would we strike. Two am was a good time to hit the trashcans—late enough to make sure that all the partiers were fast asleep and early enough to avoid the Ben Franklin types. You know the guys and gals who do the early-to-bed-and-early-to-rise kind of thing. Although I did hear that old Ben didn't follow his own advice, anyway we got to be patient, lie low for a little while and wait for the time to strike."

Carrie then swooped down from her soaring high in the stratosphere. "We struck too early. That's all. Adam simply wasn't ripe enough. His flesh—and ego—need to take a beating before he'll listen."

"Well, then, it's settled. We'll just bide our time for a while and wait for the right opportunity," I said, relieved that my crew had dealt with present defeat and seen an opportunity for future victory. "Let's see what goes on below us."

Adam could hardly contain himself. He tapped his fingers nervously on his desk, glanced up at the clock every five minutes or so. "Man, all I want today is for five o'clock to come. No, make it five-thirty. I've got to make sure the office is cleared. On Friday nights, Connie often stays until five fifteen or so getting everything organized for Monday morning. Now, I've got to lie low." So, Adam puttered around his office. More than once he went over to his private bar to make sure all his allies were ready. "You know what they say," Adam hummed in his version of Gregorian chant, "candy is dandy, but liquor is quicker. I'll bet Frannie likes those sweet fru-fru drinks with cutesy-pie names like Tropical Bliss, booze blended with pineapple juice, nectar of mango, and a dozen other saccharine confections." Finally, when Adam sensed that Connie had long since left, he called Frannie into his office. "It's been a long, tough week, Frannie. What would you like for a TGIF celebration?"

Her reply stunned Adam. She just said, "Scotch neat—no ice, just a single malt Scotch." Adam poured her a double and did the same for himself. As he did so, he turned his back to Frannie and whispered to himself, "This is gonna be easier than I thought."

When he handed over her drink, he mustered the best business voice he could under the circumstances, "Now how can we configure the crowd scene?"

"In the foreground next to you, five types should press around you."

"Yes, but which five types?"

"All the usual suspects," Frannie stated matter-of-factly as she took sip after sip after sip of her drink. Adam did like wise, only his small sips rapidly became gulps. Then she startled Adam with another burst of independence. "I need a refresher. How about another drink, Adam, the same?"

"I was hoping you'd say that. This week has parched me." Adam rose, went over to the bar and poured out two double Scotches, smirking in anticipation of his conquest.

"Hey, look at what Frannie is doing," Sly roared. She opened her purse and furtively poured out her drink into a plastic baby bottle and then sealed it tight. "She hasn't been sipping at all. She's wise to this game, I'll give her that."

"I'll wager she's playing the old Russian Bride scam," Al shot back.

"What's that?" Amanda asked.

"Well, according to my sources," Al responded slowly, trying to lend a little gravitas, to his pronouncements, "The old Russian Bride trick goes back to the days when many Russian marriages were arranged affairs. Sometimes the bride hadn't had much contact with the groom and sometimes the bride was married off to an old lecher whom she loathed. On the marriage night, the wily Russian bride would enter into a kind of unofficial drinking contest with her new husband. The old husband would foolishly assume that his innocent bride was free of guile and that after a few drinks would be amenable to his advances. They'd begin with a toast to their marriage. The bride would sip; the groom would gulp. Then the woman would feign draining her cup. When the old lecher turned to pour another round, she'd pour out her booze into a convenient spot, like a vase. Then the process would continue for round after round after round--as many rounds as were needed until the old geezer would pass out."

"Yeah, Al, but there are no vases in Adam's office, so how will she be able to pour out the booze?" Sly interrupted, annoyed that Al was stealing the spotlight.

"We'll get to that," Al retorted. "Anyway, as I was saying, the bride would then unbutton her clothes and look disheveled. When the groom awoke from his stupor, he would behold his bride in disarray and, beaming with joy over his 'accomplishment' might ask, 'How was I?' The bride would awaken from her light sleep and mumble something like, 'You were magnificent—just as I had hoped.' Then, of course, the groom would break into a lecherous smile. Some wily brides could keep up this trick for years, hoping to bide their time until they would be merry widows."

I've got to admit I was impressed, so were Amanda and Carrie. Only Sly found something to complain about. "I'll bet you got that story when you responded to some e-mail ad hyping sexy Russian women for some kind of Buy-a-Bride scheme," Sly sneered.

Al shrugged off Sly's snide comment. "No, as a matter of fact, I was taking a World Folklore class when I read about this under the heading of Tricks & Deceptions. My next class will be one on Jacobean Drama."

"Well, aren't we smart, Professor Al," Sly snorted.

"Let's get back to work, my friends," Phil thundered. I think that Al is on to something. Maybe we've all misjudged Miss Frannie."

We had. As soon as Al turned his back to pour another drink, Francie furtively opened her purse, which she had nestled in her lap, and poured the drink into a small plastic container. She did this three times before she excused herself to use the bathroom. As she turned and walked on what appeared to be wobbly legs, Adam felt that his mission would soon be accomplished and gloated before he poured himself yet another drink. When Frannie returned from pouring out her booze, Adam sat on his cherry wood chair with leather upholstery, his head hanging back, supported only by the wooden front of his office bar and his tongue resting between his lips. Soon he would be snoring. She took out her phone and snapped three pictures of her boss. Then she took a selfie, which included her passed out boss sitting in his throne and of her standing rigidly with lips pursed in disapproval. She glanced at her watch, set the alarm for two hours. I guess she figured it would take that much time for Adam to come to at least momentarily. Then she tried to sleep in another chair, leaning her head against the side. At best her sleep was fitful, so grew tired of the vain attempt to sleep and glanced through some papers on Adam's desk. All she really noticed was that some of the letterhead mentioned RYJ. "I'll have to make a mental note of that and look into it later," she whispered. She didn't want to risk ruining her own act. So, she waited impatiently for Adam to stir a bit, figuring that he would open his eyes and be awake enough for her to complete the finale to her act. Frannie unbuttoned her blouse and unfastened her bra and reclined back in her chair with half-shut eyes but only after she had taken pictures of the whole scene. In two hours, Adam had slept off enough of the alcohol to rouse himself and go to the bathroom. When he returned, he found Frannie buttoning her blouse and smoothing out any wrinkles. True to form, he asked how was it. Francie faked a bit of a swoon before replying, "Magnificent, just as I had expected, but I've got to be going."

"Do you need a ride home?" a still groggy Adam inquired.

"No, I'll be fine. See you on Monday," she shot back.

"But, what about the TV spot? We've got to finish that."

"No, we're good, I've got all of the revisions. No need to worry."

Adam was too busy gloating to worry. As she left, he turned to his bar for another drink and muttered, "Mission Accomplished." Then he downed another Scotch and resumed a deep sleep interrupted only by his snores.

"I've got a feeling that soon Adam will be paying a price for his supposed night of lechery," Amanda concluded.

"Maybe then he'll be more receptive to our warnings," Phil Added.

"Yeah," Al added. "But all of this makes me wonder what Adam's sidekick—the black clad one named Guy—is up to while Adam is playing Caligula."

"There you go again, showing off your knowledge. So how many correspondence courses are you taking, Al?" Sly sneered.

"Four," Adam curtly responded.

I wanted to keep the peace, so I suggested—actually more like ordered—we zoom in to see what Guy was up to.

"So, as I see it Guy recruits bloggers to write for his cause and then they recruit other writers, right. So, it's a typical pyramid scheme only instead of sellin' stuff, they're promotin' ideas, right?" Sly smirked a bit, assuming that he had all of the answers.

"Not quite," I responded. "Guy put a new twist on an old idea. Let's see him in action."

Just after a protest against fossil fuels, demonstrators were still mingling, talking to each other and exchanging ideas and affirming the sanctity of their cause. A few were carrying crudely written posters announcing, "Carbon No, Earth Yes," "Fossil Fuels Should Be extinct," "End the Oil Oligarchy," or simply the acronym "EOO" for End the Oil Oligarchy. A few still chanted "E-O-O, E-O-O, E-O-O." Guy mingled with the crowd almost invisibly until he spied a likely recruit, a young man of college age—perhaps a dropout—who wore a new T-shirt with EOO printed front and back with a large green globe in the front. His jeans were ragged at the bottom and stained with dirt or grease or some other dubious dark brown substance. He sported sandals, expensive leather ones, that were worn with heavy use, no socks. Hi face was bright and he beamed in triumph, trumpeting to no one in particular, "You know, this time I think we pulled it off. We're on the verge of a new era."

Guy, dressed in his usual black outfit, strolled over to him and casually struck up a conversation. "I hope you're right. The end is near."

"The end of what? I'd like to know," Sly commented.

Carrie cawed and informed her colleague, "The end of the earth."

"Yeah, so why is that?" Sly retorted.

"Because of pollution, global warming that kind of stuff," Al said. There's some truth in what they're saying. The wetlands have shrunk, and things are getting worse."

"And the jungles in South America and Africa are giving way to cattle pastures and other things," Phil added.

"Well, is solar energy the answer," Amanda asked.

"Maybe, but you know the old saying, 'Don't put all your eggs in one basket.' A complex, multifaceted problem deserves complex, multifaceted solutions. If you don't think things through, you might just be trading one set of problems for another." I rubbed my chin and wondered if humans were up to the task. I hoped so, for the fate of my species and others lies in their sometimes greedy little hands. Let's see how Guy works, first."

"Were you in the demonstration?" the young man asked. "I'm Jack, Jack Merriweather. And you're—"

"Guy, just Guy. It may strike you as a bit odd, but it's a French given name, like Guido in German or Italian. I'm glad to see you so hopeful."

"We almost tripled the number of demonstrators we had in previous rallies." Jack boasted.

"Yes, I noticed quite a crowd. I thought it numbered almost seventy-five."

"So, how long have you been in the movement?" Jack asked.

"Almost from the inception. The message is spreading even to the halls of Congress."

I don't know. I think those representatives and senators have been bought and sold by big oil."

"Not all of them. Have you heard of Senator Bobby Wainwright?"

"Yeah," Jack replied, drawing out the word as if to convey a little doubt and suspicion. "Isn't he the one who uses that old song, 'Aquarius, Let the Sun Shine In'?"

"He's the one."

"Is he for real? A lot of politicians talk the talk during election time and then spend the rest of their term taking bribes from Big Oil."

"Not Senator Wainwright. Check him out. He's the real deal. He's been pushing solar energy for years and is trying to make the federal government at least go solar in all of its buildings. He's introduced four bills in Congress to do just that."

"I didn't know that."

"Most people don't, Jack. They just think that all politicians are corrupt and in the pockets of the big companies. Some are, but not all. With this election coming up, we've got a chance to turn things around, institute a new order. Here, I tell you what, let me buy you some coffee and a bit to eat." Guy extended his hand in friendship. Jack took it.

The two walked over to a diner nearby, one of those relics from an earlier era downtown. At first, Jack nibbled on the Danish that Guy had ordered, but soon he was chomping down voraciously. "Jack, how about a hamburger or veggie burger to wash down that Danish, you know dessert first and then the sandwich."

"Yeah, great, I'll have a veggie burger with fries."

"Done." Guy signaled the lone waitress for two veggie burgers and more coffee. She brought them over. "Look, Jack, I know of a way for you to work for the Cause and make a little money in the process. Are you interested?"

"How?"

"I'm guessing that you're the type who loves nothing better than advancing the Cause, the one we're both interested in promoting.. You can work for the Cause and make some cash—only to defer expenses, of course—by blogging for Senator Wainwright. I've got all the campaign literature here. We need to build up grassroots support and the best way to do that is by having bright young people like you in our corner convincing other bright young people that Senator Wainwright is the real deal. Are you interested?"

"Yes, but—"

Before Jack could finish, Guy handed him a wad of cash, all in five-dollar bills as the waitress eyed them suspiciously. Guy noticed her prying eyes and announced loudly so she could hear, "This is like a signing bonus. Write for us and things will be right for you." That message seemed to assuage any misgivings the waitress may have had. Guy left silently, but only after he had slipped Jack some of Senator Wainwright's campaign literature as well as the cash.

Jack Merriweather whispered to himself, "Finally, my dream has come true. I can save the planet and make some money in the process."

Up on the cloud, Al shook his oversized head. "I've got to give Guy some credit. He's a smooth operator. But that Jack fellow's dream job may devolve into a nightmare. There's something else, too. Do any of you remember anything distinctive about Guy's face?"

"Nothing, not a thing," Carrie declared. "It's as if he doesn't have one."

"Yes," Amanda seconded, "his face is a blur and blends into the background."

"Well, face or no face, this Guy fellow is still working' the old pyramid scheme, "Sly pronounced. "I knew it from the start. This Jack M- will write a few pieces for ole Senator Bobbie. Then he'll recruit others, bloggers just like him, and in the process will be shoveling' in mounds of cash for each writer he suckers into the game. 'The more things change, the more they stay the same,' so the saying goes."

"Not quite," Phil observed. "I've been keeping my eye on Guy as well as Adam. He recruits writers one-by-one, so they don't know who else has been recruited. It all has the appearance of independent bloggers acting solely altruistically on behalf of the great cause. It looks as if there's a groundswell of support from the grassroots on up."

"That's a good twist," Al interjected. "They also don't know who's getting paid and who isn't. A lot of them probably know in their heart of hearts that there's something a little fishy about taking the money, and these bloggers don't want to be the first ones caught if anything goes belly up."

"A few of these so-called independent bloggers have formed informal networks. These guys read each other's blogs so it figures that these networks will form. Still, Al's right. I haven't seen any of them writing about the money they're receiving under the table. They're all maintaining and creating the illusion of simply being ordinary citizens expressing their political views. It's a relatively low-cost way of campaigning."

"Yeah, Phil, you're right," Sly admitted. "I hear those TV spots cost a bundle. And, besides, it looks as if now more people spend more time on the internet for more hours than they do watchin' TV. Yeah, Adam and Guy are into something, all right."

"So now, Adam must be thinking that he and Guy have outwitted everyone. Adam thinks he's some kind of grand stud-master and the Senator's campaign is rolling along on wheels of cash." Al swung his enormous head from side to side and did the same with his ponderous tail. "We're dealin' with some real smooth operators."

Amanda shook her head, circled around three times and then curled up in a tight ball. "Sometimes humans are too smart for their own good."

GREENER PASTURES

Adam slept off the booze until nine am Saturday morning. Frannie had long since left, so he was free to indulge his own fantasies. We all five watched him from above. Amanda shook her head in disgust. "I think I can sniff the booze-breath even way up here. And some people say that dogs smell bad. Ew! What foul stink."

"You're right, Amanda," added Carrie. That booze-breath, as you say, exudes the foul decay of death. Soon he'll be ripe enough for one of my species."

"Yeah, alligators would stuff the corpses of their victims deep in some hole in the swamp and let the flesh get nice and putrid before they feasted on it. It's not something I'm proud of, but it's the nature of things and of my species."

"I don't know," Sly interjected. "But I still think for pure rot and decay, nothing beats an old, rusty dumpster that's been sittin' for a week in the blazin' summer sun. That way the garbage gets thoroughly cooked and offers some of my species some fine eatin.' You can tell if a meal is good by how much belchin' and burpin' and retchin' goes on afterwards."

I had heard enough of such dietary discourse, so I refocused my group. "Look at Adam down there. Now he's got a smirk on his face that stretches a mile wide."

"Nothing can be so foolish as a male's ego, and that goes for dogs as well as humans." Amanda pronounced

"Yeah, the male of any species spends a lifetime in delusion," Al added. "I used to think I was big stuff, the king of the swamp until a couple of alligator hunters turned me into leather for boots and purses and steaks for barbeques and stews. But you know, I think I'm better off being humbled a bit."

"Death is the great equalizer," Carrie cawed. "The great leveler of all, man and beast, fowl and fish."

"Hey, you guys, this is getting' morbid," Sly declared. "Maybe we ought to laugh off Adam's foolishness. Look at him now." Sly pointed a forepaw to the scene below.

Adam belched and retreated to the bathroom. We aren't positive what he did there because we can't observe there without special permission (or if the door is left open). But I think we all knew what he was doing. I got a rush order for special permission to view, and it was approved with no questions asked. Adam opened his bloodshot eyes and peered into the mirror. Instead of being disgusted, though, Adam broke into a lecherous grin. "I've still got it. After all these years and all those Scotches I've still got it. Hell, I've been doing this for over twenty-five years and I'm the master of it." He stumbled his way over to his leather chair, buttoned his shirt and pants, smoothed out the wrinkles (at least the ones in his clothes) and smirked. "You know Frannie was good, not great but good. I deserve better, someone a little younger and a little bustier. Yeah, it's time to move on to greener pastures. And I think I can find what I'm looking for at this afternoon's rally." Adam checked the weather forecast. "Great, a high of 70 with almost zilch chance of rain. The rally can proceed at the park. A crowd will come out if only because the weather is so good. There will be all types of Eco-bimbos for me to check out and then add to my scorecard."

Then Adam headed for his cell phone. He carried two of them. One was a throwaway that he reserved for his calls to Guy. "Hey, Guy, how are things goin'? Did you get any more recruits?"

"Yes, Adam, all seems well. I added another blogger. His name is Jack Merriweather and he's already dashed off a piece about Senator Wainwright as the new Messiah. He's just the type we need."

"So, how many bloggers all told have you amassed?"

"Sixteen are the beneficiaries of our largesse; another thirty have been inspired by these sixteen, so we've got forty-six bloggers in total, all singing the praises of Senator Wainwright. What's even better is that of these forty-six, thirty are so dedicated and indebted to our largesse that they'll write practically anything I tell them to."

"So, how many votes do you think that will translate into?"

"That's hard to judge. A lot of people will go to rallies when the weather is nice and chant this and chant that and seem to be all hyped up but then these same people don't take the time to vote. It's always hard to predict what the fickle crowd will do."

"Say, Guy, during the rally will you do a little scouting for me?"

"The usual?"

"Yes, you know what I want."

"No problem. No sooner asked than done."

Adam sat down in his chair and eased himself back. "Things are going well, very well. Better than I had anticipated. He checked his text messages. Most were just instant deletes, but one caught his eye. "Your shipment is coming," the text stated. It was from JR Services, an office supply company, but not really. JR Services was really a money laundering service. The text let Adam know that Guy had received another influx of cash to do more work.

"I just wanna know one thing," Sly queried from his perch on the clouds. "And that one thing is how do you know about this JR Services thingamajiggy? I mean, this Adam guy does have an office and he does need supplies from time to time, so what's the big deal?"

I exhaled a bit as if I were explaining a math problem to a most reluctant seventh grader. "Well, Sly, when you wander off after one of our meetings, I do research. This JR Services does have an office and a small warehouse, only nothing is in the office, not even a computer, and nothing is in the warehouse except empty boxes. People do come and go from its empty offices but often at night and seldom during normal business hours. I checked out two of the guys who sometimes come and go. They're executives from the Let the Sun Shine In Company, the front for RYJ industries in China. RYJ uses JR Services to fund all types of activities the Chinese company is promoting, activities such as Senator Wainwright's bid for re-election."

I looked at Sly, who gave me and the rest of us a puzzled look, shifting his eyes back and forth. I don't think he wanted to admit he didn't understand what I had just told him. "OK, I get it," he stated.

Amanda turned her head away so that she wouldn't display what the humans call an eye roll. Carrie flapped her wings and Al showed his teeth as he sunk down into the clouds.

I had to get the group refocused on the subject of our study, Adam. He obliged us by checking the weather forecast and proclaiming to no one in particular. "This afternoon, it's going to be sunny, not a cloud in the sky [except for the one we'll be watching from], 68 degrees, a perfect day for a rally in the park. And rally we will."

The rally would be held in the same park, where the night rally had taken place. The weather was gradually turning colder, and it was getting a little too chilly for an open-air night rally. We watched Adam arrive at the park half an hour ahead of time to make sure that all was in order. The band was already there, setting up sound equipment and warming up, Senator Wainwright wanted his theme song, "Aquarius, Let the Sunshine In," played three times in a row to open the rally. While the band was readying itself for its performance, other people were setting up tents, some displayed glossy campaign flyers with Senator Bobby basking in the warmth of a the sun, while behind him American flags framed him in a patriotic glow. Other tents featured vendors selling hot, mulled apple cider, apple pie, pumpkin muffins, and the usual fries, hot dogs, and hamburgers, and popcorn. One tent served cotton candy and gave free balloons to children. For some of the adults, there was even a tent with a big screen featuring college football games. "Yeah, we got to take care of the adults as well as the children," Adam had advised at a planning meeting for the rally. "I mean, the kids can't vote." A few spectators had strolled in early and sampled the fare. Adam scanned the growing crowd and was pleased. "Just as I had hoped. All is going well."

Guy was already surveying the crowd, looking for new prospects— both bloggers for his work and young women for Adam's. As usual, he assumed a vantage point on the fringe of the forest, where he almost blended in with the dark trunks of the trees, camouflaging himself with the falling oak leaves. He nodded towards Adam, indicating that all was in order. Adam returned the nod and watched the crowd intently, making notes about the demographics. "Good, a lot of people, maybe seventy per cent, are twenty-five to fifty. They're the ones most likely to vote. And maybe twenty percent are over fifty. That crowd even outvotes the younger one. Some of the ones will recall the Fifth Dimension's song and reminisce about their youth. The remaining ten percent are younger than twenty-vive, maybe college students."

Even though, the young crowd numbered only ten percent of the total and had the dubious distinction of being the demographic least likely to vote, Adam seemed disproportionately interested in them. Amanda yelped indignantly, "We all know why Adam is scouting out the young crowd. Look at him, smirking, and then there's Guy spying likely prospects. What a disgrace!"

Guy motioned towards a slender girl with long brown-blond hair. She was wearing cutoff denim jean shorts, and a green, form-fitting sweater with a blue globe centered on the back. She seemed cut off from her friends. When Guy signaled her out, Adam moved in. "You seem lost. May I help you?"

"Oh, it's just Tina and Alexa. They're wandering off somewhere. They do this all of the time. They'll find me soon enough. I drove them here."

"Well, if you need any assistance, I'm here to help."

"So, what are you, some kind of Good Samaritan or something?"

"You might say that. Actually, I work on Senator Wainwright's campaign, helping to set up events like this one. By the way, my name is Adam. What's yours?"

"My friends call me Billie."

"You mean like Billie Jean King?"

"Who's that? Anyway it must be pretty cool working on the Senator's campaign and all. So what else do you do? I mean besides talking to pretty girls and all."

"I lobby other members of Congress on behalf of solar energy projects."

"That's cool. Hey, maybe you could help me out. I've got a school project to do, one on solar energy. Do you think you could get me a brief interview with the Senator? My professor will eat it up."

"Absolutely, just stay with me until the band stops playing and the Senator stops speaking." Looking into her sky-blue eyes, Adam added.

"Don't worry. We've advised the Senator to keep it brief. No more than three minutes."

"And does the Senator usually follow your advice?"

"Always. Say would you like some cider or a Coke?"

"A Coke."

"Done." Adam walked the ten paces over to the concessions and bought two Cokes.

"You know," Al wondered. "Something just isn't right. The girl talked about her professor, but the two girls she was with both had on West High sweat shirts, and one, the one named Tina, I think, looked young, maybe fifteen or sixteen, tops. My guess is that Billie isn't much older than that. She's old enough to drive but probably not older than that."

"Sometimes it's really hard to tell the age of female humans. They can use all types of stuff to make themselves look older or younger than they really are." Amanda observed.

"Yeah, but you know what they say, 'Be careful what you wish for, 'cause you might just get it' Old Adam wished for someone younger than Frannie, and maybe he got one." Sly parted his lips in a lecherous grin.

When returned to his lady love (of the moment), she was texting on her phone. Still texting, she looked up at Adam and said. "Oh, thanks. It looks as if Tina and Alexa have found their own rides home. I guess I'm left here alone."

"I can hang with you for a while," Adam offered in the most sincere voice he could muster. "Come on, I'll introduce you to the Senator and you can get his autograph."

"That would be great. Thanks so much."

So, the couple sipped their Cokes and basked in the warm sun of a fall afternoon. When the Senator had finished speaking, he worked the crowd, shaking hands and even giving occasional hugs. Soon the Senator worked his way to Adam. "Great work, Adam. The crowd is behind me. Another rally like this one and the election will be mine."

Billie burst in, "Oh, I hope so, Senator. We've just got to save the earth. And solar is the way to go."

"So who's your friend, Adam?"

"Senator, let me introduce you to Billie. She'd love you to autograph her campaign literature."

"Gladly," the Senator betrayed a sly smirk as he hastily signed one of his own flyers and added "To Billie." Then he strode off to shake more hands, pat a few more backs, and, when he deemed it appropriate, hug more supporters.

"This is awesome," Billie exclaimed after the Senator had left. "No one else in my class will have this.'

"Why don't we celebrate with a little dinner after the rally has broken up?" Adam suggested. "Nothing fancy, maybe just some pizza."

"This is awesome. I'd love to." So the two walked around and waited for the crowd to disperse as it slowly did. When they both felt assured that no one was looking, they found each other's hand.

"Wait a minute," Amanda observed from her cloud perch. "Adam just has to realize how young Billie is. She may look nineteen or twenty, but she acts just like a high school girl. How can a crafty, wily, experienced middle-aged man get himself onto the brink of disaster?"

"You know, Amanda, you're right. But I think old Adam has done the sexual predator thing for so long that he doesn't know how else to act. He's a victim all right, but a victim of his own habits. He'll rationalize his actions and justify them in his own mind."

"It's a death wish. I've seen it before," Carrie added.

"Wait a minute, you guys aren't gonna let this Billie girl off the hook, are you? I mean, it's not like he's forcing her or anything. She, too, has gotta sense that she's flirting with disaster." Sly had risen to Adam's defense.

Amanda stomped the ground indignantly and let out a muffled yelp. "Sly, don't you dare defend what you know is wrong. It takes humans a long time to grow up—so long that a lot of them never do. What Adam is up to is just wrong, no if's or but's about it. It's true that she is setting herself up to be easy prey, but she's still too young to know what she's doing."

"Well, somebody has to help her grow up," Sly meekly replied as if he knew he was wrong but had to defend his argument.

"Sly," Al interjected, "you can't even convince yourself that Adam is doing the right thing. Just admit for once that Amanda is right and that you have made an error in judgment."

"Yeah, yeah, yeah, I screwed up again," Sly finally admitted.

When no one else remained in the park and the two were alone, Adam massaged Billie's shoulders and back. "I know a pizza place, one of the best in town. I'll drive there because I know the way."

I knew where Adam was headed. The pizza place Adam referred to served an all right pizza, but the street scuttlebutt had it that it did a brisk business in serving booze to underage kids. My best guess is that's where Adam was headed. He was.

Adam escorted Billie to a remote corner of the pizza den and ordered a large deluxe pizza and two beers. Billie downed the beer a little too enthusiastically, almost chugging it. It did take her two times to drain the glass, but drain it she did. Adam ordered a second round of beers. She drank a little slower this time, but she still drank it down enthusiastically. Then Adam ordered a third round for Billie but none for himself.

"Aren'tcha goin' to join me?" she asked sloppily. She wasn't used to drinking—that was clear. I don't know much about Billie's background, but she was no experienced boozer.

"Don't forget, Billie. I'm driving."

"Oh, that's just so good of you." Billie concluded as she took a drink from her third beer. When the pizza came, Adam ordered her a fourth beer. This time she sipped it slowly but was feeling warm and a little woozy. But she still finished it. When the two got up to leave, she fell against Adam's side and clung to him as he supported her on the way out. Adam helped get in the car and positioned her in the back seat. Then he drove back to the park and the rest, as they say, is history. He waited with her until she sobered up enough—about two hours—so that she could drive herself home.

"Oh, my God," she exclaimed, "it's almost eleven. I need to get home."

While Billie downed breath mints and redressed herself, she directed Adam to where her car was parked. He did make sure she had sobered up enough to drive slowly back. He never asked her for her last name nor for her telephone number.

When she had driven out of sight, Adam gloated. "Things are going well, very well."

That evening, Frannie checked out the pictures she had taken of Adam alone and of the two of them together. "I think I've just guaranteed myself a job or, better yet, a great letter of recommendation that will get me a job far better than old Adam could ever give me. Yes, things are going very well, indeed."

THE FRUITS OF LOVE

"SO FAR, SO GOOD," ADAM convinced himself. One weekend, two scores, and those were both with younger women. Hell, I'm not getting older. I'm getting better."

From their cloud perch, Amanda stomped her right forepaw in protest. "Just who does he think he is? I once had a human owner like that. He just thought he was all that. Then he crashed his car and couldn't take care of me. Then I went to a nicer home, where the humans treated me well. For me, his accident was good—for him not so much. He should have listened to our warnings. Maybe they were a little corny, but they were also true."

"Just wait, Amanda, his story is far from over," Phil advised.

"Yeah, what comes around, goes around," Sly added. I shook my head ever so slightly and wondered if Sly were coming around, too. I guess we'll see.

Adam had slept in late on Sunday, enjoyed a leisurely brunch, watched a little football, drank a few beers, and basked in the warm glow of self-congratulation. "Hell, I'll even head to the office a little early, just to see how the other half lives. Monday morning he arrived at the office even ahead of Connie, who was never late. My guess is that she enjoyed the time alone to get everything ready for the workday without any interruptions—but that's only a guess. Anyway, Adam strode into the office with an exaggerated exuberance. When Connie followed a few minutes later, he burst out of his office and boomed out a "Good morning, Connie," before he sequestered himself again in the privacy of his own private lair.

"What's with the old guy?" Connie mumbled to herself when his office door had closed securely.

Frannie came next and headed straight towards Connie's desk. "Connie, would you book an appointment for me to see Adam at 9:30?"

"Well, let's take a look here. Yeah, that's fine. 9:30 it is."

"Good," then Frannie stomped off to her desk.

"Just what is goin' on here?" Connie whispered to Beth, a co-worker who had been gone on vacation. "I'll bet it's got something to do with last Friday night. I put a stop to this workin' overtime bit a long, long time ago. But that Frannie girl had a look in her eye that meant trouble. I'll bet that ole Adam got a little handsy and now is gonna have his hands full."

But for now, Adam sat smugly in his chair, unaware of the brewing storm. At 9:03, the first winds began to batter his smug complacency. His phone rang. It was Senator Bobby Wainwright. "So Adam, what do you want to hear first: the bad news or the really bad news?"

"Just ease me into it, Bobby. So, what's the bad news?"

"Haven't you read the morning news? My challenger is trying to rip off my environmental base. He's come out in favor of wind energy, not solar. He claims that it's more efficient than solar."

"Is it?"

"Very funny, Adam. How the hell should I know? Anyway, he staged a big press conference yesterday with all kinds of hoopla announcing his new plan to fund wind turbines all over the state. I'm tellin' ya, he's trying to steal my base."

"No big deal, Bobby. You can just call him a Johnnie-Come-Lately to the environmental issue—somebody who's desperately trying to grasp at straws blowing in the wind."

"Yeah, but I don't know shit about whether wind or solar would be a better energy source. I mean sometimes the sun doesn't shine and the winds don't blow."

"Don't worry about it, Bobby. Let your staffers do the research. You just keep the course. Hell, you could even appear magnanimous and congratulate your opponent for finally seeing the environmental light, even if he's doing so out of desperation. Just laugh him off. Your own base is secure."

"Yeah, well, Adam, you can't just laugh off the next news. You remember Lorraine, the African-American head of Human Resources at Let the Sunshine In?"

"How could I forget her? She's curvaceous piece of pure ecstasy."

"Yeah, and you just couldn't keep your hands off her?"

"Who couldn't?"

"Look, Adam, months ago when I told you to take a look at the assembly plant. Lorraine was so busy with hiring that she put you on the back burner."

"What the hell do you mean, Bobby, by saying she put me on the back burner?"

"I mean that she didn't forgive and forget. Look, when you went to check out the plant to see we could push the Made-in-America angle, you couldn't stop there. You had to check out Lorraine, too."

"Yeah, so what?"

"Yeah, so you got a little handsy."

"No problem, Bobby. No witnesses. It's her word against mine."

"Yeah, well, our source of money doesn't regard it that way. Even the threat of a sexual harassment suit against someone associated with me is enough to set them off. The last thing they want is bad publicity for the Let the Sun Shine In Company. Lorraine didn't forget; she just prioritized. Now that she has time, she took you off the back burner and tossed you into the frying pan."

"Bobby, I just don't see it that way. If she presses too hard, we'll buy her off just like we've bought off others."

"You just don't get it, do you, Adam? I know it's hard for you to believe, but there are some people that can't be just bought off. My bet is that Lorraine is one of them."

Adam leaned back in his chair. "I'll handle it, Bobby. I'll just say that it was all a misunderstanding. If I have to, I'll shut her up with a little cash. Hell, I may even offer her a personal apology, nothing public, just a quiet personal apology."

"Yeah, Adam, you'd better come through on this one. Any bad publicity could invite the prying eyes of reporters, who might be taking a real careful look at just how American-Made are the solar panels that Let the Sun Shine In assembles. I mean all they do are two spot welds and tighten six screws. Everything else comes pre-packaged from JYR back in China."

"Bobby, I've got it all under control. Call me back in a week when things have calmed down a bit. Just remember: don't sweat the small stuff."

"It's not the small stuff I'm worried about."

"Just take it easy. We'll talk next week. Ciao" Adam hung up the phone "Hell, what is wrong with that bitch!"

I thought that Adam was beginning to sweat the stuff that wasn't so small after all. So did Amanda, who shot me a look that all but said, "Adam won't be able to schmooze his way out of t his one!"

Then, promptly at 9:30, Connie called him. "Adam, your 9:30 appointment is here."

"Yeah, yeah, let her in." Just before his office door opened, Adam mumbled, "Now what can that bitch want?"

"Frannie strode in and halted just two feet in front of Adam's desk. "Adam, about last Friday."

"Look, Frannie, it was late, we were tired from the work week, we both had a little too much to drink, and things got out of hand from there. I hope that incident won't interfere with our working relationship."

"It won't as long as you co-operate."

"What do you mean by *co-operate?*"

"I've got some pictures to show you." Frannie reached into her purse and drew out the two photos she had taken. She displayed first the one displaying Adam clearly drunk in his office chair, his head slung back, his mouth half-open and his tongue hanging out ever so slightly, his shirt and belt unfastened.

"Yeah, so what's the big deal? Lots of guys in my position get blasted on Friday night. It's not like I killed somebody in a DWI accident or anything. What's the big deal?"

Frannie didn't respond. All she did was to takeout the second photo, the one showing her standing next to her drunken boss, the couple a study in contrasts. Francie appeared utterly composed and business-like, not a wrinkle in her outfit, not a hair out of place. As for Adam—well, he looked like an ageing geezer who didn't realize when he had had enough.

"What kind of bull shit is this? You were drunk as hell."

"No, Adam, you were. I was stone cold sober. I had taken only a few sips. The rest I had poured into this little container."

Adam sat paralyzed for a moment. He gritted his teeth. Then rested his forehead in his right hand.

From above, Al half-opened his mouth and commented on the scene. "My bet is that Adam can't figure out if he's more upset about a woman half his age beating him in a drinking game or about possibly facing a sexual harassment suit. Finally, after a few agonizing moments, still looking down at his desk, Adam replied: "All right, Frannie, what do you want?"

"Oh, I won't be greedy. I won't even go public—yet. I'll even generously extend to you two options. You can hire me on full-time and pay me eighty per cent of what you make or you can write me a letter of recommendation and make sure I get a job with another lobbying firm and make at least as much as that eighty per cent of what you earn. It will be easy to tell. I'll determine the exact dollar amount once I look at your tax returns from last year. In a spirit of magnanimity, that eighty per cent figure won't even include all the cash you get under the table."

"All right. I'm going for option two. I'll have the letter of recommendation ready to go by noon and make a few phone calls. You'll get your job. But right now I just can't say exactly where."

As Frannie paraded out of his office in triumph, Adam slunk down in his chair utterly defeated.

While Frannie and Adam were hashing out their settlement—actually she had dictated the settlement—Connie was talking to herself. "Well, I expect that in a few minutes, Frannie will come out, trying to hide her tears. And old Adam will be grinning away like he always does."

But this time Connie was wrong. This time the woman strode out in triumph while Adam was left choking back tears in his desk. "Well, I'll be," Connie exclaimed. "Maybe it's about time." Of course, Connie didn't know about Frannie's little blackmail scheme. Still, it's hard not to think that Adam was getting what he deserved.

Up on our cloud perch, Amanda almost howled in glee, "That old goat is getting what he deserves."

"Yeah, sometimes it's good to see the hustler hustled," Al added. Sly didn't say anything. Carrie pronounced, "Vanity of vanities, all is vanity."

Then, just before noon, after Adam had written his letter of recommendation, and made a few phone calls, he received another call, this one from his Saturday night fling, Billie. "Oh, Adam, I'm so glad I found you. I think I'm pregnant."

"You're what!" Adam cried.

"You heard me, I'm pregnant."

"I heard you, but how do you know?"

"Girls just know these things. My mother's going to kill me."

"How old are you?"

"Seventeen."

"Oh, hell. Hey, look, there are ways of taking care of these situations."

"You mean an abortion?"

"Yeah, well, maybe so, but first you've got to be absolutely sure that you are pregnant."

"I just know. What am I going to do?"

"This is Monday. We had sex on Saturday night. You're good to go for the Morning After pill."

"But it's not the morning after."

"Don't worry. They just call it that. It's good for like four or five days after."

"Where do I get it?"

"Just go to a pharmacy. They'll fix you up."

"You're sure?"

"Don't worry, Billie. I'm sure."

"You sound as if you've done this, like, a million times before."

"Just a few."

"What if I want to keep the baby?"

"Look, Billie, you just told me that you're seventeen. How are you going to raise the kid?"

"Well. My mom could help—that is if she doesn't kill me first. You know the two of us could raise the baby together."

"That wouldn't work, Billie. I'm not the fatherly type."

"Well, you could pay for the baby."

At this point, there was a dead silence—I can't resist the temptation—yes, a pregnant pause. "Billie, you need to see the pharmacist."

"Could I get a pregnancy test there, too?"

"Haven't you done that already?"

"Well, no."

"But you're sure you're pregnant?"

"Well, not absolutely sure."

"Billie, go to the pharmacy, get a pregnancy test, and, if you have to, the Morning-After pill."

"That's all you're going to tell me?"

"That's all."

"All right, I'll go. I can use the half hour for lunch and the ninety minutes for trig class which I can cut if I have to. That will give me two hours. I can even go out to lunch. My mom will call me out sick."

"Billie, I thought you told me that your mother doesn't know."

"She doesn't."

"But she'll call me out. She does it all the time."

"Just do what I said, Billie, and things will be all right."

"Yeah, all right. Say Adam, can we see each other next weekend?"

Adam paused. He almost blurted out something—probably something like "I don't think that would be a good idea" but he checked himself and did what he'd done before. "I'm out of town next weekend on business."

"All right. See you later. I'll call you after I've seen the pharmacist."

"Yeah, sure. Bye now." Adam hung up the phone and rested his forehead in his hands. "How could I have been so damn stupid?"

Up above, all five of us looked down, thinking the same thought: now would be a good time for our third apparition. I got all four of my colleagues together and announced. "Now is the time to strike. All four of us will make ourselves visible to Adam, one by one, and advise him."

"But, Phil, we haven't planned anything," Al objected.

"Well, Al, we tried the scripted version and that didn't go over well. So, let's just do it. I'll go first. Maybe Adam will even remember me."

I took shape in front of his desk and glared at him. "Adam, now is the time to make things right."

"Oh, hell, you must be some type of hangover hell. What the hell do you want me to do? Marry the little girl?"

"No, I just want you to stop treating people as scoreboards of your ego. That's all."

"Get the hell out of here."

"I will, but we won't leave you alone."

Then Amanda surfaced. "Don't think you're better than a dog. Prove that you've got a soul." Then she disappeared.

"What the hell is this, a three dog morning?"

Al came next. "Even the meanest predator in the swamp will eventually get his come-uppance. You've got time to prove that you can be more than an ageing predator. Otherwise, the predator will emerge as the prey."

Sly came nest. "Hey, pal, I know from experience. Even the craftiest can get out crafted. Learn a little humility. Your street smarts won't always work."

Finally, Carrie appeared, making a grand entrance, swooping down and perching on Adam's desk. "Death is the only certainty. Your only option is to kill your old self and rise anew. Look ahead at your own funeral. Who's there?"

Adam gazed out into a vision of his solitary death and funeral. Still he remained unimpressed. "I need a double Scotch. The only way to beat a hangover is to get a little drunk again,"

Up above, Amanda lay down in apparent defeat "I guess we didn't make much of a difference."

"No, Amanda, we didn't fail. Adam did. Who knows, maybe in the end our words will make a difference. No one can argue that we didn't do our best." I was trying to convince myself as well as Amanda. Still, Adam's reaction disappointed us all. But Adam was making a habit of disappointing people.

ACCCUSATIONS, DENIALS, DENUNTIATIONS

At NOON, CONNIE CALLED AND asked Adam if he wanted to make reservations for lunch. He grumbled something about not leaving the office and not receiving any visitors, especially any women visitors. "What the hell has gotten into the old goat?" Connie responded, quite secure that her boss couldn't hear anything.

"Yeah, what has gotten into the old goat?" Sly echoed from above. "I, for one, think maybe, just maybe, we've made some headway with the old guy."

"I hope so," Amanda added.

"Well, we can't rush to judgment," Al replied. "The guy is a lifelong predator and he's gonna find it hard to change, maybe impossible. He's the type who on his deathbed will be trying to grope the nurse who's trying to help him get his bedpan out. I've seen gators like that in the swamp, old guys with rotting teeth and bloated stomachs, still prowling around and trying to swish their tails as if they were young."

I just told my colleagues to be quiet for now and just observe what old Adam is thinking. The lawyer and lobbyist hung his head low and supported it with the palms of both hands. He maintained this pose for several minutes. Then he raised his head, exhaled, and said out loud: "Maybe I ought to stop drinking. What the hell-- talking animals scolding me as if they were preachers! The next thing you know I'll be seeing pink elephants. No delirium tremens yet, just plain old delirium.

Anyway, let's see how Guy is doing." Adam whipped out the phone designated to call Guy only. No answer. ""That's all right, he'll call me back in a couple of minutes." Adam waited for ten minutes. No call. "He must be tied up or something. It's not like him to not get back to me."

Sly licked his lips. "I, for one, think the old goat is sweating it now."

"Don't rush to judgment, Sly. All it will take is some victory, big or small, for Adam to revert to his old self."

That victory came about fifteen minutes later. Connie said that a young woman named Billie was on hold. "She said it was important. Do you want to take this call, Adam?"

Suppressing a rush of air from deep down in his chest, Adam did his best to come off as casual. "Yes, I'll take it."

"Adam?"

"Yes, Billie, what is it?"

"I'm not pregnant. I took three tests in the bathroom at the pharmacy and all of them turned out negative."

"Are you sure? Do you know how to read the results?"

"Adam, I'm not stupid. There are only two options, both clearly labeled. One on the right says 'Pregnant' and one on the left that says 'Not Pregnant.' And every single time I was over to the left." Her voice trailed off at the end. I wondered if she felt disappointed either about not being pregnant or Adam's thinking that she was dumb or maybe a little of both. But she bounced back quickly. "Hey, Adam, is there a rally this weekend? We could go and, you know—"

"No rally, Billie. In fact, I've got to go out of town this weekend on business and may not be back for days."

"Oh, Ok, I just thought, I mean, you know we could."

"Not this weekend."

Sly couldn't contain himself. "Nope, not this weekend and not forever. Ole Adam is just puttin' her off until she'll forget about him. I mean, what was she thinkin'? Adam was going to be her prom date? He's dodged a bullet—"

"Yeah, Sly, he has, and I'll bet he'll back to his old ways tomorrow."

"Some humans never get it, do they?" Amanda pronounced.

Carrie, who had been quiet so far, broke in with her raspy voice. "Even at death, as the spirit is leaving, he'll be the same old Adam. Oh,

I've seen deathbed conversions, but those are few and far between. One's life often dictates one's death. Not always. I've witnessed good people writhing in agony and others, lifelong devils, pass assay quietly in their sleep. But that's the course of Nature. And Nature is neither cruel nor kind nor just. Just utterly indifferent like the blazing sun in the desert bearing down on bleached bones in the sand."

Carrie's lengthy discourse took me by surprise. Al summed up all of our sentiments. "Yep, for Nature there's no such thing as just desserts. Some win for a while. Some lose. But it makes no difference what they've done or what they haven't done. It's all about survival for the moment. Some have long moments; others die at birth. It's all the same for Nature, which is no mother. In fact, a lot of the time, she's just a mother—"

"You're right, Al, but let's see what Adam's up to." Amanda concluded.

Adam lounged backward in his chair. "I think it's five o'clock somewhere," he concluded, and went over to his private bar and poured himself out a double Scotch on the rocks. "But maybe I oughtta lie low for a while. You know, take it easy."

That afternoon, Adam's office hummed along as if nothing much had happened. Then around four o'clock, Connie called Adam, who by now had poured himself a few more double Scotches. "Adam, Frannie called and said she got the job at JJ Worthington and won't be back."

"Time for another victory toast," Adam declared from the sanctity of his private office. "This may be my greatest day, getting rid of two bitches in one day."

From above, Amanda stomped her forepaws. "Phil, why are wasting time on Adam. He's just a reprobate, as intransigent as a granite mountain."

"Well, Amanda, I guess we're supposed to give the old guy every chance he can get, but you're right. I don't see him going to a monastery or anything to atone for the error of his ways." I shook my head and then knuckled my way over to a new perch on the cloud base. Scratching my chin, I added. "But who knows? There may be little hope for him, but perhaps on a grander scale things will turn out right."

Down on earth, Adam was feeling warm and woozy. "I'll sleep it off here in the office and then head home for a shower." He buzzed Connie and told her that he would be working late and didn't want to be disturbed.

"Yeah, right," Connie remarked. "He's probably gone off on some binge and wants to sleep off the drunk. He was doin' his darndest to keep from slurrin' his words."

So, Adam snoozed, possibly dreaming of new conquests.

But Tuesday morning came quicker than Adam had hoped.

At first, Adam still was feeling the effects of the previous day's alcohol. He walked into the office still in the throes of a boozy somnambulant state. Connie just shook her head, as she had grown accustomed to this behavior from her boss. "Coffee, Connie, please, and lots of it." These occasions marked the only time Connie fetched coffee for her boss, figuring that the benefits of taking pity on his impaired condition outweighed any other considerations. When Adam was sober, Connie told him to "Go get your own damned coffee, Mr. Albright." By ten o'clock, Adam had recovered enough to get his own coffee. But then Connie knocked twice on his door. "Mr. Albright, I think you'd better see this right away."

Half joking, Adam asked, "What is it, some kind of warrant?"

"Not quite, but it is some kind of legal document. Look at the envelope."

"Just hand it over, Connie." She did. After a momentary pause, he said a little too loudly, "You can leave now." Connie exited and Adam was left alone to contemplate his thoughts. "It must be from that Billie-bitch. She's smarter than I thought. She's probably going to extort hush money from me."

From on high, the five were assessing the situation. Al spoke first. "You know, I think Adam is expressing what he would have done had the roles been reversed. He'd ask for hush money."

"Isn't that like prostitution?" Amanda asked rhetorically.

"It's the way of the world, baby. That's the way it is," Sly commented, arrogantly affirming his own worldliness.

"All roads lead to death," cawed Carrie.

"Let's not draw any premature conclusions," I intoned. "Let's just wait and see.

"Well, it's not from Billie or Billie's attorney," a relieved Adam said out loud, assuming he was secure in his own office. "It's from an attorney representing Lorraine Bledsoe. Who the hell is Lorraine Bledsoe?" Adam sat for a few moments, mutely perplexed. "Oh, yeah, now I remember. She's the African-American Human Relations guru at Let the Sun Shine In. Yeah, Ok, so I made a pass at her. So, what's the big deal? She told me to get my hands—actually she said paws—out of her pants. And I did, a little slowly maybe but eventually I came around. She wants me make a public apology for my behavior or she'll initiate a sexual harassment suit. Damned if I will. I'll just deny the whole affair and denounce her as trying to come on to me. In the end, it's a he –said-she-said affair. No witnesses, no crime. No big deal." Then scanning down two paragraphs, Adam gulped. "Hell, she quit Let the Sun Shine In and took another job. She's going to go public, claiming that the Made-In-America claim is bogus. Who the hell initiated this, some political operative?"

"Yeah, Phil, who got old Lorraine started on this and why did she wait so long?" Sly wanted to know.

"I'm not sure, Sly. From what I can ascertain, Ms. Bledsoe was so busy at first hiring qualified veterans and checking out their credentials that she may not have been aware of what was really going on at the plant. Then, when the hiring frenzy had ended, she had a little time to observe what was really going on at the factory. She probably thought that Adam was just a jerk and brushed off his advances. But, when she saw that the only manufacturing going on was doing two spot welds and tightening a few screws before putting the solar panels in pre-fabricated boxes, she saw a pattern of deception and conceit."

"But, didn't the president deny the accusation?" Sly asked.

"At first, the president said nothing, as he was probably waiting for orders from China, but then Guy wrote an official press release that denied any wrong-doing and insisting that the solar panels were genuinely American made by American veterans."

Sly smirked furtively. "Ok, Phil, I can see what's comin'. Adam's thinking that the letter was just a form of dirty trick from a political operative probably has some truth to it—after the fact, of course. By now, old Senator Bobby Wainwright's opponent in the election has sent down swarms of reporters to investigate Lorraine Bledsoe's charge. Now that she landed another job with another company, she's free to speak her mind. And, once she starts talkin' the game may be all but over."

"You're probably right, Sly, but in a few hours of human time let's scan on over to the factory to see what's going on," I insisted. So, the four waited until three-thirty human time at the plant where the solar panels were assembled. The workers were headed out to their cars. Three different reporters approached the workers and asked if they could interview them. One declined the offer and slammed his car door shut, revved up the engine and took off. But the other two agreed to talk for a few minutes. "So, what do you guys think about working at Let the Sunshine In?" the reporters asked. The two gave the same response. "It's great that the place hires veterans. Some of us moved here just to get the job. The pay is good and the benefits are out-of-sight good: free medical and dental and vision and a pension plan. Just how many places offer a pension plan any more, I ask ya?" Then the reporters asked if there were any drawback. The two gave the same answer: the job was boring as hell; all they did was tighten a few screws and do two spot welds. Then some other guys put the panels in boxes and loaded them onto trucks. That was it, day-in and day-out, hour-in and hour-out, the same old thing. The reporters thanked them for their service and for their time to answer the questions.

Swishing his massive, powerful tail, Al commented. "Now Adam is gonna face enemies on two fronts from two different angles: harassing women and lying to the public. What's he gonna do?"

The answer came the next morning, when Senator Bobby called Adam, who by now had sunk into a deep depression. "Senator, what are you gonna do?" Adam let out a whisky-whine after twelve hours of trying to drown his troubles.

"Oh, come on, Adam, don't be so thin-skinned. If you weren't so busy chasing women, you'd know exactly what to do: for every accusation there's both a denial and a denunciation. You should know, you've been doing the same thing for years, even decades. Sober up and get busy, denying and denouncing. In the mean time, I'll have Guy look into my opponent's dirty deeds."

After he hung up the phone, Adam sobered up enough to assess his situation, getting no answers but asking the right questions. "So, now Guy is working directly for old Bobby. Is that why he hadn't returned my phone calls? Anyway, I'll ignore Lorraine's accusation until it comes time to deny it. Then I'll accuse her of coming on to me. As for Let the Sun Shine In, I guess that's the Senator's problem I'll deny any connection to the company and claim no knowledge of what was going on there."

"I guess old Adam's got it all figured out," Sly observed. "Ya know, though, I think Lorraine's gonna be a lot tougher to deal with than was Bobby. She's got another job, so he can't threaten her with job loss. Ya know, for all we know, her current boss, whoever that may be, could even be encouragin' her to go after Adam. I don't think the guy has made many long-term friends, if ya know what I mean."

"I hear you, Sly, and you might just be right," I commented.

It took a few days for word to get around that Lorraine Bledsoe was going to pursue sexual harassment charges against Adam Albright. On Thursday of that week, having heard nothing from Adam, she filed a sexual harassment lawsuit against. She wanted no money, only a public apology. "You can't buy me off with money," Lorraine announced. "No money will make up for what he did to me. I just him to acknowledge what he did to me and possibly to other women won't happen again."

When Lorraine Bledsoe made that announcement, she invited other victims to come forward. First Frannie joined in the chorus of outcries, declaring her experience, although conveniently omitting her Russian Bride ruse. "I want to join with my sister in pain, Lorraine Bledsoe, and declare publicly how Adam Albright abused his position of power and pressed me for sex. I was so shattered by the experience that I had to leave my job and look elsewhere for employment. He deserves to be exposed. I invite all victims of his predatory sexploitation to come forward and make their case known." The dam of denial and repressed memories had broken. Next Pilar, a community outreach advocate, came forward. "Adam Albright told me he wanted to know how he could improve Senator Wainwright's standing in Hispanic neighbors. He wanted a private talk so they wouldn't be disturbed. He took me to his office after work hours and tried to get me drunk. Then he rubbed my shoulders and tried to work his way down. I slapped the bastard and stormed out of his office. Before now I thought that I was the only victim of this sick mind." Then Hillary followed suit. She was a school superintendent, whom Adam asked to interview. He had seen her on television and claimed he admired her efforts to expand opportunities for disadvantaged students. "Then this Mr. Albright tried to take advantage of me," she declared. "But I would have none of it, so he continued to press me, literally. Only when I threatened to go public with his unwanted advances did he stop. I know now that I should have gone public right away so that other women wouldn't have to suffer the indignities that I had." Then May, a Taiwanese-American accountant, came forward. "I thought that Adam Albright was just one of those white loners who had caught yellow fever, daydreaming of supposedly compliant Asian women. I told him repeatedly to leave me alone. But the phone calls still came. He still pressed my hand a little too forcefully on those public occasions when I had to meet with him. Then one time when he found me alone, he pressed me against the elevator wall and tried to fondle me. I slapped him, pushed him away, and got off four flights short of my destination. He should be ashamed of himself." Finally Billie joined in the outcry, describing how Adam had plied her, an underage girl, with beer to try to get her to have sex. She left out the part about fearing that she might be pregnant.

"Now, why do you suppose she did that?" Sly asked. "I mean wouldn't that make her case of sexploitation stronger?" Sly asked.

Amanda was quick to respond. "Sly, she feared her mother's wrath more than she feared anything else."

"Oh, yeah, I guess so," Sly responded with humility unusual for him.

The next blow came from Senator Wainwright, who had been fuming all week, before holding a press conference and formally distancing himself and his campaign from Adam Albright. "I formally disavow any connection to Adam Albright, a man whom I foolishly respected. He deceived me just as he had fooled other victims of his deplorable scheming. Had I known of his reprehensible behavior with women, I would not have allowed him to campaign on my behalf."

"So now even the Senator is playing the victim angle," Al commented. "Neither one of the two will man up."

"Do you think it's time for another apparition," Sly asked. "I mean, maybe now the creep might be more receptive."

"Not now," Amanda responded. "Let's see Adam's next reactions."

I was astounded at Sly's behavior. Most of the time he was a prankster, but he never hurt anyone but himself. Maybe I shouldn't have just dismissed him as a clown. Still, he could be really annoying.

Abandoned by his staunched ally, Adam stayed late in his office. As Connie left work that morning afternoon, she wondered if she had contributed to his lechery "Maybe I could have come out, too, But I slapped the SOB, told him my husband would kick his ass if he ever found out, and that was that, or maybe it wasn't."

Alone in his office, Adam called Guy on his private phone. "Hey, Guy, I was wondering if you could help me out here."

"Don't call me again, Adam. We're through. I've got work to do, so don't harass me. But you've got to look at it this way, Adam. At least you're an equal opportunity harasser. You've got African-American, Latina, Taiwanese, and white women all denouncing you. Now that's an accomplishment. Good-bye and don't call me again."

Adam just sunk down in his chair with a few tears making their way down his cheeks, but none of those tears were for anyone else, just for Adam.

CROCODILE TEARS

Two weeks had passed. Accusations had been made, denials issued, and violent denunciations thundered across the media. Every day Adam walked into the office, and every day the mood remained somber. One by one four staffers had exited. At first, Adam seethed. "Oh, so what's-his-name left for greener pastures. Well, he wasn't much good anyway. Good riddance and take your two weeks notice with you. Get the hell out of here." Taking their cue from the anonymous what's-his-name, three others left silently, just leaving an e-mail message stating that for personal reasons they were leaving. "Go on, get out of here," a somewhat subdued Adam voiced quietly. "I can save some money." He felt that, if he and Connie could weather out the storm of criticism raining down on him, that he would make it through this temporary tempest. But then it happened. The first hint that the storm wasn't passing was the handwritten letter from Connie. Adam read it to himself out loud. "Dear Mr. Albright, the two of us have worked together for many years. We've shared many experiences, both good and bad, but always weathered the storms together. I know that you are a strong-willed man and will eventually walk away from this current controversy. However, I have been offered a very lucrative position with full benefits and, with two children both in middle school, my husband and I have been wondering just how we could shoulder the increasing financial burden of children who will soon be needing money for college as they mature into adults. So, reluctantly, I am giving you two weeks notice. I had thought of seeing if you could match the salary and benefits package I have been offered, but I decided against that approach as it would appear as if I was simply leveraging the two competing offers against each other. Besides, I have personal reasons for wanting to leave. I just do not think I could work in an environment in which you and I would be the only ones left in the office. Even if this situation would change, the environment would not be healthy for either you or me. Accordingly, I am submitting my resignation and giving two weeks notice."

"What the hell does Connie mean by saying that the office environment would be unhealthy for both her and me? Haven't I always treated her well? We had a little spat at first, but after that incident I left her alone and the relationship between the two of us remained strictly business-like. I guess she's thrown in with all the other women who are screaming for my speedy castration. Well, she can go to hell along with the others. The vultures are circling overhead, licking their beaks or whatever the hell vultures do in anticipation of feasting on my rotting corpse. Well, let them circle for as long as they want. They'll soon tire of it all and I'll be up and at them again. Go to hell with the rest of them and take your two –week notice with you. I don't need any of you, not now, not ever. I don't want to see your smirking faces any more. I can face this tidal wave of betrayal and criticism alone. I don't need a one of you." Adam slammed the door to his office and sulked alone.

Up above, Al broke the silence. "You know, I could almost feel sorry for the guy. He's never known what it's like to be absolutely alone with nothing but his thoughts. He's always had a crowd of people stroking his ego and now he has none. Still he deserves whatever he gets. I have a feeling that he'll never sincerely repent, that, if it's not about him, then it's got to be about nothing."

"You're right, there, Al," Amanda responded. "It's always been about him. Now he'll have to live with the consequences. Do you think he'll change?"

"He might, and it's till our duty to see what we can do. We might be paying him a visit but not yet. He still stands defiant. I wonder what he'll do next?" I asked.

"With all due apologies to Al and to his crocodilian confederates, I'll wager that Adam will be shedding a few crocodile tears to see if he can garner at least a little sympathy. A lot of guys like him send out waves of pseudo-apologies when all they're doin' is tryin' one last trick to get some sympathy and support. I've seen it all before," Sly confessed. Amanda shot him a look that all but said that Sly had practiced the same trick. Sly shook off the non-verbal accusation and went on. "Of course, sometimes those crocodile tears can be mixed with real tears, too. We can't rush to judgment."

"No, we can't," I concluded. "Our mission isn't finished just yet."

"I don't think that Adam has given us vultures much credit. We can sniff the smell of death long before our prey final succumbs. The vultures are, indeed, circling overhead, but they can be patient far more patient than any human, for they realize that the only certainty is death."

"Didn't that old guy Ben have something to say about death and taxes being the only certainties?" Sly added.

"Yeah, but hustlers like Adam have figured out all kinds of ways to avoid taxes. In fact they've gotten so good at avoiding unpleasant consequences that they've convinced themselves that they can avoid death." Al turned his enormous head slowly from left to right, taking in a panoramic view of his colleagues.

"I guess you've summed up the problem, Al," I responded. "It's going to be tough to make any changes. Still, there have been deathbed conversions."

"But not often," Carrie added.

"No, not often," I had to admit.

"But it's still possible," Amanda said.

But down on earth, the judgment had already been made. In the court of social media, Adam had been accused, tried, and convicted. In his case, however, the court of public opinion had called it correctly. Six credible accounts from six credible witnesses, none of whom knew each other, so there was no possibility of collusion. Some might argue that Frannie herself was guilty of extortion; nonetheless, she was acting in self-defense. Billie was too young—a paradoxical naïve seductress. However, I think there's no point in splitting legal hairs: Adam still acted as the primary predator. Lorraine Bledsoe, May, Pilar, and Connie were blameless. Adam had invited the torrent of criticism that rained down on him.

And the deluge of condemnation fell from the heavens, not for forty days—hardly any scandal can last that long anymore; there are far too many of them and the media critics, both professional and amateur, soon tire of he same provocative, salacious story and move on to another one equal or greater in titillation. Across Twitter, Facebook, and other social media outlets critics called Adam an amoral crib robber, a pederast, a sexual predator, a menace to civilized society. Others, a bit more savagely inclined, called for his immediate castration, perhaps an open-air pubic spectacle in a stadium. Others argued that impalement would be a more effective deterrent. For many public flogging was in order. Others demanded sensitivity training, mandatory sexual harassment courses (that is instruction in how not to harass rather than how to. For some individuals the "how to" part comes naturally as a part of their genetic make-up so it would seem). Many insisted on restitution—especially financial restitution. Many lawyers generously volunteered their services to those who wished to pursue legal action in civil courts. All that Lorraine Bledsoe called for was a public apology.

Faced with the torrential onslaught, Adam sat alone in his desk. He would soon lose his desk, his office, his condo and everything else that was mortgaged. So, faced with no other option, Adam tried his last resort: a tearful public apology and a vow to seek mental help for his sexual addiction. He set up a press conference, but by the time he did so interest in his crime story had waned and the public and the press corps, for the most part, had moved onto the next scandal of the day. Still, Adam had rehearsed his performance so often that for him, at least, it was a momentous event. Two reporters, both from local radio stations, had casually strolled in. Even though the two were competitors, they nodded to each other in recognition as Adam mounted the three steps to the podium he had set up in the empty space once occupied by Frannie, the intern. "Thank you for being here," he forced himself to say. Then, turning sideways and shielding his eyes with his right hand, he paused for effect as if overcome with emotion. Then he gradually turned and looked out on his audience, who had witnessed similar scenes in the past. "I know now that my behavior has been offensive and has violated the trust between two human beings and for that I am genuinely sorry." Here he turned away form the crowd, took out a handkerchief and wiped his eyes, red and swollen from having been rubbed. "I realize that no amount of restitution can make up for what I have done." Here he paused again as if grasping for words.

From above, Sly commented. "I know what old Adam is up to. He's trying to cover himself from civil suits. He don't want to pay out any money. Of course, it's doubtful that he'll any money to pay out now that no one wants to hire him and his rat-faced friends have deserted him. Oh, yeah, it's over."

As if pulling himself away from fierce demons tormenting him, Adam faced the front and gazed out to the end of the room, looking past the two lonely reporters who dutifully listened to his spiel. "I've started therapy for this fierce, self-destructive addiction that has seized my soul and driven me to behavior repugnant to civilized society. That I did not seek help sooner, I admit and for that I am sorry. I can only hope that with the help of my therapist, I can find my way to a new self. Thank you for your time." When he had finished, his little speech, he turned abruptly away and locked himself in his office either because he couldn't face his shame in front of the crowd of two reporters or because he didn't want to answer their questions. The two looked at each other for a few minutes, shrugged their shoulders, and lamented the fact that they had at most thirty seconds worth of material for their evening broadcast.

Al commented rather laconically, "The guy played the victim angle and it didn't work."

Sequestered in his office, Adam wrote down on his legal pad one last option. "Call Guy and throw myself at his mercy, beg for a job, any job." So, he used his throwaway phone to call. "Good," Adam pronounced when the phone rang, "Guy hasn't gotten around to changing his number."

"The answer Adam got didn't offer any consolation. "Look, Adam, I've told you once and I'll tell you again. I'm through with you. I've got bigger fish to fry. I'll change my number if I have to, but whatever the hell you do, don't call me again." Adam was crushed.

The real press conference, the one that garnered multiple reporters some from out-of-state, concerned Senator Bobbie Wainwright. The questions that reporter after reporter hammered away at the Senator all involved one core issue: what was the Senator's connection to the now disgraced lawyer and lobbyist, Adam Albright? The Senator clung to one central response, one that he hoped would resonate with the voters: "I was taken advantage of by a crooked lawyer and lobbyist. I have severed all relations with him and dismissed him from my campaign team." When questioned about Adam's encounter with an underage girl at one of his campaign rallies, the Senator was equally adamant. "I had no idea, absolutely none, that Mr. Albright was intent on seducing the young lady. I did see them together, but assumed that he was simply talking with her about politics and environmental issues. I assure you that in no way did I have any knowledge of this sordid affair until it went public." When questioned about his lack of prudence in placing so much trust in someone like Mr. Albright, the Senator had one pat answer: "My relationship with Mr. Albright was strictly business. I had no knowledge of his personal life. If I had, I would have immediately distanced myself from him and severed all ties—both of which I have done upon knowledge of his reprehensible behavior. I assure you that in the future I will screen all of my associates not only for their professional credentials but also for personal behavior."

The next question probed into other matters. "Senator, it's rumored that you have invested heavily in solar energy firms. Is the rumor true? Old Bobby didn't skip a beat. "I'm glad that you asked that question. As we have all seen from this most recent scandal, a public figure's personal life is just as important, nay, even more important, than her or his stand on the issues. I have placed all of my financial matters in a blind trust managed by a professional team. I know little about my financial matters. They do, however, give me a weekly allowance. That's about all I know."

Then one reporter changed topics: "Senator, your opponent in the election shares your concern with environmental issues; however, he favors wind energy as a viable alternative to fossil-burning fuels. What do you say to that?" Senator Bobby paused for a moment and then replied. "I welcome, another ally in the environmental cause but I do question his timing. Some have called him a Johnny-come-lately to the environmental cause. He must have seen my recent polling numbers and decided to come aboard and join us. For that I welcome him. But my staff researched the whole matter of wind energy thoroughly before recommending solar energy. While it's true that in the Great Plains and coastal areas of the US, the wind blows constantly and may provide a steady source of energy, here in the Midwest the wind is as reliable as the weather. We all joke that we can experience four seasons in one day. In the morning it's chilly, cold even. But no wind. Then the weather shifts and it's spring-like and then the temperature starts popping into the nineties. For us, the sun is far more reliable than the wind. It does get blustery at times, but wind energy demands a constant flow, not a bluster here and a bluster there. Without that reliable source, we would be freezing in the dark of winter or baking in the glare of summer."

From above, Al spoke almost admiringly of the Senator's performance. "Well, the old guy certainly knows how to work the press. Just like Adam, he lives a double life: publicly he's the dedicated servant of the public; privately, he's the dedicated servant of his ever -increasing wealth. Like Midas, everything he touches seems to turn into gold. Unlike Midas, he never directly concerns himself with whom he dehumanizes in the process. He distances himself from just as he has distanced himself from Adam. He's the alpha predator in the murky swamp of politics."

"Yeah, the guy knows how to hustle, that's for sure," added Sly.

Amanda wondered, though, if he could weather the current storm of controversy about his relationship with Adam Albright. "Do you think he can still win the election?"

Before responding to Amanda's question, I had to pause for a moment and think things over. "I'm not sure there's any winner here, Amanda. His opponent doesn't seem any better than he is. It seems to me that the environmental issue is both a political and an engineering issue. The politics is all talk; the engineering is the action part. And action should take precedence over the empty words of politicians. In any event, it looks as if everyone wants to save the planet but no one wants to shut off the air conditioning. Let's see what Guy is doing."

Guy was busy having his team of bloggers research the viability of wind energy. I said *team*, but maybe that's the wrong term for none of the bloggers knew each other. Guy was intent on maintaining the appearance of independent, concerned, patriotic citizens acting on their own to express their sincere convictions. And, I guess, some of them did. But Guy kept the money trail well hidden. No one on his *team* knew who else was getting cash payments under the table. In doing so, although they'd never admit it, they were complicit in Guy's scheme. While the matter was never stated, they each understood, that the more they advanced the Senator's cause, the more money they got. And each one thought, that he or she was the only one getting paid to be a professional activist on behalf of the Senator. Guy's little scheme had all the appearances of a simultaneous, grass roots movement while in reality it was all carefully orchestrated by Guy himself. And besides, as Guy bragged privately, "It's a hell of a lot less expensive than TV spots."

"How long till Election Day?" Carrie wondered.

"Well, next week is Halloween and the week after that are the elections," I responded.

"Which one is scarier?" Amanda asked.

DECISION TIME

"I DODGED A BULLET, DIDN'T I, Guy!"
From his vantage point in the clouds, Sly turned his head and then blurted out "What Bullet? I know what a bullet feels like: first there's a loud bang and almost at the same time a bloody impact that knocks you down, sends you plummeting from the tree down below where the coon hounds yelp."

"Yeah, Sly, down in the swamp I felt the same thing, first the explosion above me and then almost at the same time the explosion inside of me. But I got a general idea of what the Senator is talking about. It's Election Day, and so far he's managed to steer the reporters away from the one issue that could metaphorically kill him."

"Yeah, so what's that?"

"Sly, just listen and you'll learn," I advised.

"Yeah, yeah, whatever you say, Phil."

"Don't worry, Bobby, your investments are safe with me," Guy said. You overpay me for 'consultation fees' and then I take my overpayment and sock it in a third party investment firm that then invests it in greening companies like Let the Sun Shine In."

"But, Guy, how do I know you'll eventually have dividends come back to me?"

"Easy, Bobby, you know I like to pay in cash. I'll hand you over mountains of cash, some of which you'll hand back to me so that I can reimburse our army of bloggers. It's a win-win proposition. Besides, if you can't trust me, then who can you trust?"

"I don't get you, Guy. You don't seem to be in this for the money. So, what drives you on?"

"Let's just say the thrill of the chase."

"Yeah, well, I just enjoy the rush of air when I fan the bills in front of me. Just because I've got a blind trust doesn't mean I can't pull down the blinders once in a while and take a peek. Let the Sun Shine In is making money hand over fist, but the real money starts flowing once we get my bill passed for all of those government contracts for solar panels. So, where's the thrill of the chase for you in this big money grab?"

"My Chinese associates want a far larger share of the solar panel market. Right now Thailand, Malaysia, and Viet Nam have corralled eighty per cent of the solar panel market. South Korea also takes a slice. Sure, a lot of the solar panels those countries sell ultimately come from China. They're just circumventing US customs and sanctions, but my Chinese friends are tiring of dealing with middlemen; they want a virtual monopoly and all the money and power that come with one. For appearances sake, the Chinese just want to win sixty percent or more of what they see as an expanding market."

Yeah, well, it's a good thing you advised me to stop using the 'Made in America' pitch. Otherwise, the Federal Trade Commission, jabbed by news accounts, might start looking into that claim. The best we can say is that some assembly is done in the US. You know, though, I don't think the public much cares where the production is as long as prices are low. Oh, yeah, we get a lot of mileage about saying how Let the Sun Shine In employs vets and all, but patriotism goes only so far. The bottom line is still the bottom line."

"But the bottom line for all humans is death and death alone," observed Carrie. "How does the Senator figure that in? I guess he'll have a more expensive casket and all, but the end is coming whether he knows it or not."

"Isn't that our job?" Amanda added. I know we've tried to warn Adam and failed, but maybe we should try again."

"We could," I responded, stroking my chin. "Maybe Adam has hit bottom so hard that he's healing his bruises and mending broken bones—to say nothing of his ego."

"What about the Senator?" Amanda cried. "He's in need of help."

"He is, but we're not authorized yet to deal with him. Maybe in the future. For right now, we have to concentrate on our primary mission: saving Adam Albright from himself. He might listen or he might not. It's tough to break through a shell that has been growing and growing and still growing since boyhood."

"What do you mean, Phil?"

"Well, Adam had doting parents who saw to it that he wore the best clothes, went to the best schools, then to the best universities, then to the best jobs. He was programmed for success and he did, in fact, succeed. He enjoyed so much success that he just always assumed everything would go his way. And, for the most part, things did. Not to say that he didn't work hard. He did. He always did his homework, staying up late to reread passages he didn't understand and never satisfying himself or his parents with any grade less than an *A*. He always trained his body equally hard, running and lifting and straining and pushing himself to get better."

"So what's wrong with that, Phil? He sounds like about as good as a human can get." Sly interjected.

"Because it was always about him, about his success. That's why he never had any long-term relationship with women. It always had to center around him and his success. Later in life, he kept scorecards about his so-called wins with women and with money. No matter what, it was always about him. He'd even give generous donations to charitable causes as s long as these donations advanced his self image."

"So, for the most part, he was a self-centered phony," Al judged. "Yeah, I hate to admit it, but I see a lot of myself in Adam. I worked hard to become king of a relatively obscure part of a swamp. I practiced my skills over and over and then I put my training to work. I did succeed in a small way, but now I'm in this kind of limbo-land, neither heaven nor hell, a place where all of the species co-exist—even some humans."

"Al, you're my friend here, but I don't think we'd be on friendly terms back in the material world of earth, where most animals compete for food, sex, and security." Amanda faced Al and fixed her eyes on him as she spoke.

"Well, Adam has competed so hard that he's beaten himself," I added. "Let's check on what's going on down there."

Three days before the November election, three days before decision time, the Senator busied himself making speeches and disparaging his opponent. He hammered away with the theme that his rival was a Johnny-Come-Lately to the environmental movement, an opportunist, who had no genuine interest in alternative energy—not even in wind energy that he so publicly favored. When reporters harried the Senator with questions about his possible ties to Let the Sun Shine In, he dismissed any innuendos of wrongdoing. "My finances are all handled in a blind trust," he repeated over and over again. To my knowledge, I have made no investments in any particular company and am free of any possible hint of self-interest. I'll admit that I admire the policy of Let the Sun Shine In, a policy that puts veterans first. I can only wish that other companies would do the same." He was careful to say no more about the solar panel company that really operated as a front for a major Chinese firm." Ignorance is bliss" became his motto. He also carefully avoided calling Let the Sun Shine In a "Made in USA" company, repeating again and again that its policy of hiring veterans first made it a model for other American firms.

Guy had his squads of "independent" bloggers writing frenetically about why they supported Senator Wainwright. By now his bloggers had come to rely upon Guy's ever-flowing cash as a lucrative addition—I almost said addiction—to their personal finances. Guy had thirty bloggers working for him but no more than three in any one metropolitan area. He spread out his bloggers throughout the state, so that none would suspect that they operated as a network of paid, professional, personal advocates for the Senator. His plan was working well. Guy hustled around the state so much that it seemed he was everywhere at once. No one could tie him to a specific place.

However, as we observed from our vantage point, this wasn't the case with Adam. He had nowhere to go and nothing to do—except one last futile effort to assert himself. "Whatever else goes on, I'm gonna make sure I vote against that SOB Senator Bobby-boy. And that he did. Adam sported his best suit as he went to vote. He even paid fifty dollars from his ever-diminishing funds for a haircut that acted as a throwback to his more prosperous days.

Gazing at the spectacle below where Adam stood in line with a dozen other people, all of whom must have assumed he was someone important because of his dress and personal appearance, Amanda proposed one last effort to throw him a lifeline: "Should we try one last apparition?"

"Yeah, why not?" Sly responded. "But this has got to be the last one. If he hasn't learned his lesson by now, I guess he never will."

Al shut his eyes as if deep in thought. "At first I thought another apparition would be like begging. But maybe not. Now it's decision time for Adam. He either makes or breaks himself on this one."

"What do you think, Carrie?" I asked, trying hard to cloud the issue with my own feelings. But Carrie said nothing. I think that she had already foreseen Adam's fate. Still I paused, allowing her time to speak if she so desired. She didn't. "Amanda's right. We ought to give it one last effort."

After voting, Adam had nothing else to do other than to return to his apartment. He still had six months left on his lease. "How the hell am I gonna pay my rent? I've got no job, nor any likelihood of getting one. Maybe I can beg Guy just one more time and get on as one of his bloggers. I'll have to use an alias, though." Adam sat on his bed and then rose to look at himself in the mirror. He saw an old, broken man. I could tell because he let his eyelids close halfway as if he couldn't bear the sight of himself any more. "Now," I said now is the time for our visit." My image appeared in the central part of the mirror with Carrie soaring above me. Close by my side sat Amanda. To my left Al lay submerged in cloud cover so that only his eyes and half-opened mouth were visible. To my right, Sly sat on his hindquarters, extending an accusatory right forepaw. As for me, only my huge face appeared, with eyes moistened with tears that refused to drop. I hate to admit it, but I felt sorry for Adam, who had squandered his life. "Adam, Adam," I whispered. "You still have time to change things, time to help yourself by helping others."

"So, now what are you and your troupe of circus friends gonna do, show me the grave and frighten me into becoming something I'm not?"

"Adam, you have a chance to remake yourself, be born again into a new you."

"Go to hell all of you!" Adam screamed. "Get the hell out of here. Where the hell is hell anyway?"

"You're already there," I concluded.

"Well, decision time for Adam didn't turn out as we had hoped," Al observed at our debriefing. "But you know, I don't think we lost. I just think we faced an impossible task and did the best we could."

"Maybe we can get a second chance, not at Adam, perhaps, but with someone else. I like working with you four," Amanda added.

"Yeah," Sly admitted. "Yeah, we're a team now."

Carrie cawed in approval and then took off for a brief flight.

As soon as Carrie landed, Gabe flew in. "I've got two more assignments for you five."

"What are they?" I asked, a bit astonished.

"Senator Wainwright will win the election but, like Adam, he may lose himself in his delusion of perpetual success. And then there's Frannie, who also may be losing when she thinks she's winning. I'll give you details about your new assignment later." With that, Gabe blazed off into the heavenly distance.

"All right, team, we meet again."

PART II

ADAM'S FATE

FALLING LEAVES
AND FALLING FORTUNES

THINGS DOWN ON EARTH SOON turned blustery. October's sunshine had yielded to November's dark and dreary rain. One week after the election, all the rallies had ended; the results were in. The post-election victory parties had ended; the post-election debriefings of failures had ended, too. As for me, I hate to admit it, but my own personal sense of failure lingered on. Adam was still Adam, no doubts about it. The five of us had tried the apparition-thing, and it fell on deaf ears and blind eyes. Just about the only accomplishment we could boast of was a momentary reduction of Adam's cocaine intake. Now he wouldn't have the money to buy that cocaine. In fact, he wouldn't have any money at all. His law license had been suspended for ninety days. The standing joke circulated around town went as follows (I overheard this one many a time): "We would have suspended old Adam's law license indefinitely; but, if we did that, we'd have to suspend the license of over ninety per cent of the lawyers in town." What galled Adam the most about the joke was the epithet *old*. Overnight, so it seemed, he had aged twenty years. Still, he had no recourse other than to shrug his shoulders and move on. Adam paid out the three remaining months on his lease and closed his office. "I'll be able to work from home," he argued, "and without any overhead or any lazy, self-serving staff." He made other concessions to his newfound state. "I'll cut out the dining out. That'll save some bucks. Besides, who knows better how I like my food cooked other than

105

my own humble self." Even though it was turning colder, he turned the thermostat down to fifty-nine. "I can wear a sweater—no big deal." He had to dismiss his gardener and housekeeper. "I'll have time to take care of myself and my home now that I won't be working so much." The only luxuries he allowed for himself were his home and his car, a late model BMW sports sedan. "If things get really tough, I can sell the car. No matter what, though, I'll keep the house. I could never get the same deal again." Still, when the bill for his real estate taxes arrived in his mailbox, he cursed what he called government inefficiency and corruption that had run on his tax dollars.

He cursed even more when he raked the leaves that rained down from the stately oaks that lined the one hundred foot long driveway to his mansion. He had blisters on his hands from all the constant motion of raking and he had throbbing back pain from all the bending over to pick up the leaves and bag them. "Who in the hell thought it would be a good idea to bag leaves? Shouldn't they just lie there, decompose over the winter, and fertilize Mother Earth? Isn't that Nature's way?" He might use the same argument the following spring when he tired of cutting the one-acre plot of land with a push mower he would purchase at a garage sale. "True environmentalist would swear off all of these modern propensities for a manicured lawn free of any leaves." He found housework equally tedious, if not more so. "Who in the hell has time to cook gourmet meals?" he complained after one frustrating round of trying to follow a recipe for Coq au Vin. Damn it all anyway, what it all comes down to is that it's still chicken. I'll just throw the carcass of the dead bird into the oven after sprinkling some salt and pepper and dousing it all with some cheap wine. Rosie O'Grady should do. I mean, what the hell, all the alcohol will get cooked away anyway. I'll call it Coq a la Rosie." And so Adam stumbled along, adjusting to his newfound poverty.

All of my interest and even obsession with Adam didn't go unnoticed. "You just can't let go, can you, Phil?" Gabe chastised me as if I were an unrepentant schoolboy, and in a way I guess I was.

"Yeah, Gabe, I can't. I feel as if I let everybody down. I mean there was no miraculous transformation despite everything that me and my crew did." Gabe shot me a look that pulsed with meaning. "OK, I'll admit it. It's an ego thing. I just don't like to lose. I wanted to feel my fists pounding against my chest in victory. I wanted Adam to turn around, but even more so I wanted to win. I guess it's just in my genes even in the after-life."

"Phil, if you didn't have that longing to win, you wouldn't have been chosen for one of our most difficult cases. In any event, the other archangels and I have decided upon a new strategy. You're to renew your mission to save Adam. Only this time it will be more like a reconnaissance type of thing. You are to keep an eye and ear on Adam and to intervene directly until we've all had time to see if Adam can make the right calls on his own. And your team will be limited to only you and two others. Got it?" I nodded in acceptance and off Gabe flew just as fast as he had whizzed in.

"All right," I reasoned. "If I'm limited to only two other team members, which two should I pick? Well, without money or status, Adam won't be much of a predator, so Al's insights probably wouldn't help much. Still I wonder if I can, from time to time, call upon his expertise. So, he's off. I guess the same is true for Sly. Old Adam has lost so much credibility down on Earth that I doubt he can pull off any sneaky tricks. Yeah, I'll rely on Sly just as I will on Al. The two of them can be consultants, called upon in ad hoc situations. Amanda has such a cool head and moral sense that I have to have her on my side. She's ready to lead her own pack, but I need her level-headedness. She also acts as a counter to my chest-thumping ego. So, Amanda's in. So, is Carrie. Only Death and the threat of Death keeps humans and animals alike from spinning off to self-destructive orgies. Carrie's in, as well. So, it's set. My team is ready to do that reconnaissance thing that Gabe spoke of."

Almost instantaneously, Amanda strode in and Carrie swooped down. "I understand that our assignment with a certain Adam Albright has been resurrected," Amanda declared.

"Yes," I replied.

"And that now our mission will be predominantly reconnaissance— to determine how Adam is adjusting to his new condition." Amanda added.

"Right again," I remarked.

"Well, then I am honored to serve once again," Amanda concluded. "When do we start?"

"Right now."

Carrie said nothing, but she seldom did. Her head nodded ever so slightly in assent, so I sensed that we were primed to begin our observations.

Adam was raking leaves at a pace he couldn't maintain. "That son of a bitch little Bobby-boy will pay for this. I'll rake him over the coals the same way I'm taking on these leaves."

"His hands are red and blistered," Carrie commented. "I wonder just who is being raked over the coals."

"He has heaped all of his frustration and anger on one person. That's a common human trait and, I must add, a most stupid one." Amanda lifted her right forepaw to emphasize her point.

"I've got it. I'll call those two reporters who showed up for my press conference and expose Bobby-boy for the self-serving son of a bitch he is. Election or not, his buddy boys in the Senate will throw his ass out when they learn of his ties with China." So, Adam temporarily took a break from his yard work and hustled into his house where the cell phone reception was better, so he claimed. But we all three knew that he had to go inside to take a break. Sometimes it takes humans a long time to learn how to pace themselves. He called one radio station and rubbed his aching hands and burning blisters in anticipated glee. "Boy, wait until they get a load of this," he burst out. "Old Bobby-boy is on the way out, nails in the coffin. Hell, I'll even attend his resignation speech and clap like hell." But the first station wasn't interested. All he received after demanding to speak with the station master was a perfunctory "We'll get back to you." The response was garbled in an officious way whose meaning was clear. "That's all right," Adam consoled himself. "I'll call their competitors." So, he dialed the second radio station and demanded to speak with the reporter who had attended his press conference.

"And what is the name of the reporter you wish to speak to?" the voice over the phone asked him.

"How the hell should I know," Adam fumed. "Look, just give me the stationmaster or whoever the asshole in charge is. Tell him it's Adam Albright on the other end."

"Yes, Mr. Albright."

"Well, it's about time I'm getting some respect."

But all Adam heard was an annoying buzz--a disconnect. He called back. The anonymous voice on the other end informed him that the stationmaster was out of the office and wouldn't be back for the rest of the day.

Adam knew what that response meant. He had used the same line many a time himself or rather his secretary had. "I miss Connie," Adam confessed. "I miss her a lot." And suddenly Adam felt terribly alone. He even left a text message for his ex-wife Mary DeLuca asking if his daughter Cassie and son Mike would be available for a visit on Christmas. The next day he received a curt response. "We've already made plans for Christmas, but you can stop by the weekend before for a brief visit. Make it a late morning visit. Both of them are wrapped up in their own affairs."

"I haven't seen them in months. I guess I can't blame them for giving me a second class, second rate appointment. I guess it's time to get back to raking." And rake he did, although at a much slower pace. He found some work gloves in the garage and lubricated his blistered hands with Vaseline before putting them on and resuming his task.

"Well, it's not much, but it's something," Amanda observed. Maybe the time alone with himself will make him realize that he's not good company."

Amanda was right. Adam's Thanksgiving was a glum affair. Every year for the past ten years, Adam's wife, Mary DeLuca, had invited him to share a Thanksgiving dinner with her and their two children. And every year. Adam had declined, sometimes excusing himself because he had to work—or, as he gleefully chuckled to himself, play. This year there was no invitation. The thought of roasting a whole turkey and having at least a week's worth of leftovers sickened Adam. So, he picked up what used to be called a frozen TV dinner and watched TV by himself. The pro football game was mildly amusing although he hadn't followed either team. Once the game was over, he switched channels to avoid the endless round of commentary that frequently followed each game. He had a choice: he could select the channel that would feature *The Miracle on Thirty-Fourth Street* from start to finish or he could select the channel that already had run through the first half of The *Miracle on Thirty-Fourth Street*. He chose the latter. He watched dispassionately until the end when the new family moves into a new house. Then he rose from his chair, almost tipping up the folding table that supported the remnants of his Thanksgiving feast. "This is just BS. There's no free ride anywhere. Now, if the guy had bribed the prosecutor to get the loony Santa guy off, then it might all make some sense. That's the way of the world. Money makes more money and the more you got the better you are. And, above all else, it doesn't matter how you get it— until you're caught. What the hell! No more philosophizing. Maybe I'll celebrate the occasion by getting wasted. In the old days, he would call up his dealer and snort cocaine, but he didn't have the money to do that any more. And dealers, even more than everyone else, expect to be paid in cash and on the spot He had already downed all of his best single malt Scotch. All he had left were two bottles of three-dollar wine. So, he sipped these down grudgingly, not because he savored each drop but as a form of self-inflicted mortification.

"A drunk human is half a corpse," observed Carrie, "only still farting and belching."

"He's just feeling sorry for himself," added Amanda. "He hasn't learned anything. He's still the same old Adam, wrapped up in himself and his own delusions. He's hopeless."

"Perhaps not," I concluded. "He's only undergone the first two stages of grieving for his lost glory, such as it was. At first, he was enraged; now he's sunk down into depression. There's a chance that he might just rise up, but he wouldn't do so miraculously. It's all a long, slow process. And not everyone completes it."

CHRISTMAS PAST
AND CHRISTMAS PRESENT

THE MONDAY FOLLOWING THANKSGIVING SAW a flurry of bills stuffed into Adam's mailbox. Just two months ago he had laughed off these monthly bills as petty nuisances. Not any more. The electric bill, the water bill, the sewer bill, and--worst of all--the real estate bill from the county. He paid the electric bill first, vowing to cut back on his use, mumbling something about shutting off several rooms that he no longer used. He'd even reduce the time he spent showering. "No more of those long, twenty minutes of having multiple nozzles direct streams of warm, soothing water at every part of my body. From now on, it's just in and out in two minutes or less. There wasn't much he could do about the sewer bill. "It is what it is," Adam stated to no one in particular for he had no one to talk to. But then came the real estate bill: over $16,000. He gulped when he saw that. He knew the bill was coming; he knew how much it would be. Still, the shock of seeing the actual figures in front of him caused him to gasp, put his head down, and support his sagging brain, staggered by the burden of such an assessment. After a few moments, Adam recovered. "I guess I'll have to sell the Beemer. I used to joke that I seldom drove the BMW convertible any more than ten miles a day, except when I drove it to the airport. I should be able to get more than twenty-five grand for it. I mean, it's got low mileage and is only five years old. Hell, I ought to be able to pay my real estate bill and have enough left over to pick up some hooptie that will at least get me around town. Yeah, that's it. I'll take care of that tomorrow."

"Humans just confound me," Amanda declared. "I mean, first of all, who needs over sixteen rooms just for himself? What was he thinking when he won this estate. It's not like he has family or servants living there. Now, it's even worse. He's got huge bills and the quickest way to take care of his money problems would be to sell not just his luxury car but his luxury house as well. What is he thinking?"

"It's all status, Amanda. That's all it is," I added. "The kids who would mock me by jumping up and down and making what they thought were monkey noises did so because they could feel superior to me. They knew in their heart of hearts that they were weaker and maybe not even as smart as I was. They learned the mocking game from their parents, many of whom worked for bosses that made them feel like low-life creeps. It's the pecking order thing. Adam is holding onto his mansion because he's really dreaming of winning back his old life, once his law license is restored. By my figures that should be by the first of March. He can buy a luxury, status car any time; buying a mansion similar to his present one—well, that's another thing altogether."

"Even in death, the humans play the status game. Some build grand pyramids; others on a lesser scale store their rotting flesh and decaying bones in mausoleums. Others fret their dying days wondering about their legacy. In the end, as I know so well, they're all the same—food for grubs and worms and crows and vultures and bacteria so small that even microscopes have trouble focusing In on them. Adam is no different from most humans." With that lengthy pronounced, Carrie flapped her wings and soared into the sky above.

"Carrie's right," Amanda added. "Humans even compete with each other over the dogs they own and have set up a hierarchy of dog breeds, sometimes for a practical purpose but largely just all for show and status." But here Amanda paused, turned her head to the side apparently in deep thought. "Well, come to think of it, I guess dogs are no different. There's always the fight over who will be the big dog, get the most food, and have the most sex. I guess it's just part of Nature. And Nature can be cruel, can be kind, but most of the time is just supremely indifferent."

"You're right about that, Amanda." I looked down and stroked my chin. "I did more than my fair share of chest thumping back in my material days. Maybe all of us are like Adam in some ways. Well, Adam doesn't have much status now. So, he'll cling to whatever remnant of status he has—his mansion—even if he can't really afford to keep it up. He's got sixteen rooms but will use only three or four of them: the kitchen, the bathroom, his bedroom, and a study. Still, that's more than most people have for themselves. He'll hold onto the place even if doing so kills him. As the ancients used to say, 'Fama fugit sed vanitas manet.' Fame flees but vanity remains."

"Well, what will Adam do with all of that space?" Amanda asked, still befuddled by the ways of humans.

"He will seal off a lot of them. In other rooms he'll just reminisce about the good old days."

"Phil, what do you mean?"

"You'll see," I concluded.

True to his word, Adam sold his BMW the next day, He had momentarily thought of himself driving from dealership to dealership, hat in hand, pleading for someone to pay him cash or to let him trade down for a far less expensive car. But even the prospect of such humiliation rankled Adam "No, I'll wait to go to the dealership when I'm the one with money to burn. Maybe I'll get a Jaguar. Who knows?" Humbling himself, hat in hand, in front of car salesmen would not be for Adam. He sold his car online and had it picked up in front of his house two days later. He still had to invent an excuse when the tow truck driver arrived to pick up his BMW. "I'm thinking about giving myself an early Christmas present, you know, buying up." The tow truck driver nodded in agreement and responded that he knew what Adam meant. I'll bet that the guy who hauled away the Beemer knew all along why Adam was selling it. But among humans, keeping up the pretense of wealth and status is of paramount importance.

A week after Thanksgiving, Adam found himself alone in his mansion with little to do. Oh, there would be leaves to rake; in fact, it seemed if there would always be leaves to rake for months to come. He could do some painting; but paint cost money and right now Adam shrugged when he saw the peeling walls in some of the now vacant rooms. So, he had time to dwell on the past. He went down to the basement and surveyed trunk after trunk of who-knew-what. "What the hell was I thinking when I kept all this junk?" Adam said as he gingerly made his way past the mounds of dusty trunks to one that caught his eye for a reason at first he didn't recognize. Then he realized what had drawn him to that particular trunk. "That was my parents' years ago when they both were alive and I was just a kid. What the hell could be in there?" Adam lifted the latch and slowly opened the lid. Inside a smiling Santa Claus stared at him, so did a menagerie of green-clad elves. "Just old Christmas stuff," Adam concluded. But, digging deeper, he found an old action figure missing one arm. "Yeah, I played with this all of the time," he mused, "even when the right arm fell off probably because I yanked on it so much. The oversized, inhuman musculature of the figure seemed to mock him. "You're not so strong now, but neither am I." He also found a two-foot high plastic Santa Claus figure that would light up, an outdoor decoration, and a lighted three-foot wide manger scene. "What the hell," Adam burst out. "I may as well put these out. I've got nothing else to do." Then he yanked out from the bottom of the trunk an old paperback copy of *A Christmas Carol*. "Just a load of sentimental tripe," he said out loud. "Yeah, well, I've had my share of apparitions, too, and nothing came of them."

Amanda couldn't contain herself. "Nothing came of them, you bumbling idiot, because you didn't pay any attention to them. Humans always play the blame game, but they conveniently forget to ever consider blaming themselves. Here's a smart man with plenty of potential for himself and for society, and he ruins it all. He considered only the potential for himself and no one else. I could just bark my head off at the fool and bite at his trouser legs."

"I don't know, Amanda, perhaps we could have done a better job in the apparitions department. I don't know. The world has become so obsessed with material reality that they forget other dimensions." I still felt a keen sense of failure over Adam's stubborn refusal to acknowledge us.

"It's all a matter of timing," Carrie added. "Adam had no imminent fear of death and the common fate of all things material."

Adam laid out the lighted Santa Claus figure and the manger scene. "I'll put these out after I've checked out these other two trunks." In the next one, just as dusty as the first, Adam found old report cards going all the way back to kindergarten. "My parents kept these as scorecards of my success." He flipped through the elementary school years. "All *A*'s except in art. I never could draw anything more complex than stick figures." His high school reports continued his academic glories, culminating in a full-tuition scholarship to a near-Ivy university. "I wish my parents would have taken a bite of the bullet and let me go to Princeton, where I had a half-tuition scholarship. Maybe then I would have made it even better. I would have made contacts that would have lasted a lifetime. Maybe I would have made it to a better law school."

"There he goes again—blaming everyone but himself and thinking only of himself. Did he ever think of even his parents' needs? They weren't exactly wealthy, so I understand. They must have sacrificed a lot to support their son's academic success. This guy just doesn't get it." Amanda shook her head and then did a full-body shake as if she were trying to rid herself of any thoughts of the man she had come to loathe.

"The guy is a self-centered jerk, all right, Amanda. On that we agree. But it's still early. It will take more than a few apparitions to turn this guy around. He's spent a whole lifetime cultivating himself and no one else." I added.

"You're right, Phil. Still he just makes me so mad." Amanda stomped her right forepaw down in emphasis. "Maybe putting out the Christmas decorations will be a start."

Amanda was right. After Adam set out the lighted Santa Claus figure and the manger scene, he decided to call his ex-wife. "So, what are we doing for Christmas?" he asked Mary DeLuca.

Her response rang out with a chilly stridency. "I know what your son and daughter and I are doing for Christmas. The real question is 'What are you doing.' You've missed the last four Christmas dinners on account of business, you said. You've missed out on all four years of your son's high school experience and your daughter's last years of high school and her first years of college. So, I know what we're doing. We're having our Christmas celebration as we've done for the last several years—without you."

"So, you're telling me that you've moved on?"

"That about sums it up," was the laconic response.

Up above, Amanda exclaimed, "Way to go, girl."

Back down on earth, Adam said nothing for a few seconds and then said in almost a whisper. "All right, then, I guess you've got good reason to feel that way." Adam exhaled slowly almost as if admitting his guilt.

"Look, Adam, if you want to spend Christmas dinner with the kids, why don't you plan to come a few days early. Cassie will be home from college on December twenty-second. We could have an early dinner—both of the kids will want to go out with their friends—and so will I. It will be nothing fancy, just a few appetizers and some Christmas cookies with hot chocolate, maybe around three o'clock."

Chastened by the less than enthusiastic response, Adam responded, "All right, then, three o'clock on the twenty second."

Over the next few days, Adam remained perplexed over what presents he could bring to his children. In the past, he had simply written a check, but now he had no money to give. "I've got no money to give them. I've got no idea of what to do."

From up high, Amanda looked down on the scene and shook her head in disgust. "It's not a matter of money. We could shower you with money for presents and you still wouldn't give the right presents. You'd probably buy each of them a fancy car and then they'd wreck it or couldn't afford the insurance or repairs. You don't know what to give them because you don't know them. Cassie, your daughter, has one weakness: she loves chocolates, especially dark chocolates. She loves to nibble on a piece or two during her late night study sessions. You could get her those. And Mike, your son, has one longing that he dare not tell his friends at school: he would love a bound set of all of James Joyce's works. He reads voraciously, you don't know."

"Now, Amanda, we can't expect too much from old Adam. He's got a pretty steep learning curve to make. It may take years to make him; it may take years to unmake him, months if we're lucky." I stated this all rather paternalistically, but I meant it. Maybe I had a selfish reason, too. I was still smarting a bit from that sense of failure. We hadn't been able to turn around old Adam around despite our best efforts.

"Phil, I know you're right, but I'd just like to jump up on him and bark in his face, rattle his brain into some sense of empathy, maybe even nip on his legs. He's a human, after all."

"I know what you mean, Amanda. I'd like to rattle him, too, pick him up and squeeze some sense into him, but we can't. We'll just have to wait patiently from above and hope and pray that he transforms himself into someone we can respect."

The afternoon of the twenty-second finally arrived. Adam had decided to give his children what modest gifts he could afford. Serendipitously, he picked up a box of inexpensive dark chocolates for Cassie. He remembered that her mother had had a craving for them back when she and Adam had lived together. Still nonplussed about what to give his son, Adam got him a gift card to the local bookstore. "He loved to read as a young kid. Maybe he still does." Adam was so brimming with hope that he left for Mary DeLuca's house early. His hooptie had four very worn, almost bald tires, and a cold rain had slickened the roads. Still, the journey turned out to be less perilous than he had anticipated and he arrived twenty minutes early. So, for ten minutes he sat outside his ex-wife's door. Finally he opened the door, not knowing what to expect. "I guess it won't be too rude to be ten minutes early. In the old days, I had made it a point to arrive fashionably late. Yeah, well, those days are gone, at least until I get my law license back."

As he entered the door to Mary's house, he was stunned to see how Cassie had matured. "For God's sake, she's gorgeous. She looks even better than her mother did at that age." Then Adam's mind turned regretfully to another topic. "And Carrie is two years older than Billie. What the hell, was I thinking?" He wished his former wife "Merry Christmas" and she returned the greeting. "Merry Christmas to you, Adam. Come sit down. There are cookies and a few appetizers on the table. You like shrimp, I recall."

"Yes, thank you, Mary. Here, Cassie, I've got this for you. And, Mike, this one is for you."

Then, almost in a chorus, they responded, "Thanks, Dad," as if they had rehearsed it. Perhaps they had. I don't know for sure, but I'll wager that Mary had prepped her children that their father had fallen on hard times. He had.

Adam downed shrimp after shrimp voraciously. He must have found them far more appetizing than the frozen dinners he had been picking up at the Dollar General store. Finally, he checked himself and asked his children how they were doing. Again, he received a choric response, "Thanks, Dad." They still hadn't opened their presents. In five minutes, Cassie excused herself. "My friends and I are going skating at that new indoor rink, I'd rather go to the outdoor one, but with the rain and all, we can't." Mike made a similar response only he and his friends were going to the movies to catch the late afternoon Early Bird special.

Sensing that his children had given him the cue to go, Adam rose, thanked Mary for her hospitality and left. And that was it, a perfunctory Christmas for a perfunctory father. As he put on his coat and left, he noticed the large diamond ring on Mary's finger. Once he was safely outside the door, he said to himself. "Well, she has a right to live her own life and even enjoy it. I guess I know where she and the kids are going to spend Christmas. And maybe they should"

As for Adam, he spent Christmas alone. The TV was on. One channel featured *It's a Wonderful Life* and *Miracle on Thirty-Fourth Street*. Adam watched neither one but kept them playing as background noise while he downed a bottle of cheap wine he had picked up for the occasion.

JANUARY: LOOKING FORWARD AND LOOKING BACK

"J ANUARY'S ALWAYS BEEN A STRANGE mix for me," Amanda confessed. "It's a frozen, quiet time between two years."

"Yes," I replied, eager to show off a bit of antiquarian lore. "The month gets its name from the Roman god Janus, who had two faces, one looking one direction and another one looking the other. That's the nature of January. It's part of the reason some humans sing "Auld Ang Syne," cherishing the past and then making New Year's Resolutions, looking to the future."

Back on earth, Adam was cherishing his one drink of single malt Scotch. He swirled the ice cubes round and round as he huddled over the drink. He had managed to find one bottle tucked away in the recesses of the kitchen pantry and had saved it for this special occasion. The bottle stood out, partially because his pantry had gone so bare. "I used to think that New Year's Resolutions were for losers. Well, I guess for now I'm one of those losers." He took a small sip of his Scotch before he resumed his reflection. "Yeah, I guess I am a son of a bitch for being such an absent father. I'll grant you that one. They don't even know me. At Christmas, I may as well have been the great long-lost uncle from nowhere as far as they were concerned. Yeah, I had one of those. I had an aunt and an uncle from God-knows-where who stopped by once a year and bought me a Happy Meal—even when I was fifteen and long past the Happy Meal stage. All right, I've got a resolution. I'll spend more time with my kids. You know, get to know them. All right, I've done my duty. Now where's that long-lost bottle of Scotch. There might be enough for just one more drink." There was.

He emptied the bottle and then tossed it into the recycle bin. "We've got to save the Earth, don't we." He wondered what would become of Senator Wainwright. "I know that old Bobby-boy is looking ahead to a fat pension. Just what he hell does he do in Washington anyway? Eat fancy dinners at fancy restaurants and take gifts under the table from lobbyists like me or I should say like lobbyists like I used to be. I wonder where his solar panel bill will go? I guess he'll wheel and deal and no matter what come out ahead. As for me, I've got a little less than sixty days, fifty-seven to be exact—before I can get my law license back. And then, who knows? Maybe I can go back to dining at four-star restaurants. Hell, who knows, maybe even a five star joint now and then."

Amanda shook her head. "This guy hasn't changed at all. If he had the money, he'd go right back to his old self, an old, drunken satyr. I guess a modest, temporary period of minor deprivations won't be enough to turn him around. Now I don't feel so bad about our failed efforts to get to this guy. He's a reprobate."

"I was thinking the same thing, Amanda. He is a hard case. But, what's really sad, is that there are so many just like him."

Cassie chimed in. "He needs to experience real suffering and the reality of death. He lives for a future that is rooted in his past."

For two weeks, Adam didn't do much other than to sleep in and leisurely read the news on the internet. He could still manage to pay his cable bill for internet service, but he'd have to forego cable television. When the snow fell and piled high on his driveway, he didn't bother to shovel it off. "Hell, I've got nowhere to go just now and nothing to do, so why bother? It'll just melt anyway." Years of training and practicing had shaped him as a master of rationalizing almost anything. "I've got Exactly forty-three days until I get law license back. So, for right now, I can hunker down in the three rooms I can still heat and just look to see what comes."

One day, he glanced through the headlines and, buried in a

brief report in the local news, one story caught his notice. "Senator Wainwright nominated to head the Senate Sub-Committee on Ethics."

Adam leaned back in his chair and roared, "Well, laugh out loud, ain't that a bitch! Old Bobby-boy does know a lot about ethics—about how to avoid them. Well, maybe he'll fit in well."

January also meant looking backward to last year's finances and ahead to next year's. As far as next year's, matters remained too unsettled. True, he'd get his law license back, but that alone was no guarantee of success. Adam was trying hard to convince himself—since he had no one else to convince—that all would turn out well. "All right, every day I'm getting closer and closer to having my law license back. I'll start make inquiries in February. For now, I'll concentrate on making up for lost time with my children. I used to just write a check once a month for child support and that was it. My secretary Connie handled all of the details: when to send the support check, when to send birthday cards, when to send graduation gifts, all those things. Well, I guess now it's all up to me." Adam was writing out the support check and it pained him to do so. He stopped mid-check and rested his forehead in his hands. "I don't have the money to do this. It's either support my kids or feed my own face." Here Adam paused, exhaled deeply, and continued writing the check. "I could stand to lose a few pounds anyway." He had uttered the same sentiments when he had to buy new tires for his hooptie. It still ran but moaned pitifully when he cranked it up on those bitterly cold January mornings.

"Well, for once, Adam has done the right thing," Amanda declared. "Too bad, it's years late. I doubt he can ever make up to his son and daughter for all of those lost years."

As usual, Amanda was right. Even Adam must have been thinking the same thing, for the next day he called up his ex-wife and asked for his children's cell phone numbers. In the past, Connie had tracked that information as well. Just before he called, he realized that he had other regrets. He knew where his ex-wife and children had spent Christmas and it wasn't with him. "Well, Mary deserves some happiness. I caused her enough grief." He got the cell phone numbers and even congratulated Mary on her engagement and wished her well. When he did so, there was an awkward silence on the other end of the phone call. I guess it turned out to be all right, for when it ended, Adam was smiling ever so little, but this time not for himself. "Hell, I've really screwed things up."

He phoned his son Mike first because he was still in town and asked if he would like to go out for a soda and spend a little time to catch up. The answer on the other end of the line surprised him. "Yeah, I've got a little time next Monday. We don't have school on that day. But no soda. I'm in training. I've got a scholarship offer, full tuition, for cross country and track and I've got to stay in shape."

After the call ended, Adam shook his head. "I didn't even know Mike was running. The last I knew he was playing soccer. I guess my own son is a stranger to me."

Father and son met awkwardly at Kelly's Sports Bar and Lounge. Just in case, Mike wanted something to eat, Adam stuck a twenty-dollar bill he had saved up for the event. I could tell by how slowly and gingerly he stuck that twenty bill in his wallet. He even gulped a bit as he did so.

"I'll bet Adam is praying that his son won't be hungry," Amanda whispered to me. Carrie just flapped her wings in assent. Fortunately for Adam, Mike said he wasn't hungry and ordered only a smoothie that cost $4.99. "Aren't you going to order anything, Dad?"

Adam replied that he wasn't hungry. "New Year's Resolution, you know. I could stand to lose a few pounds here and there."

Amanda observed that in this instance at least Adam wasn't a very good liar. "I can hear his stomach rumbling up here. That aroma of freshly grilled hamburgers must be driving him crazy. "I'll also wager that Mike's Mom had briefed him on the downturn in his father's fortunes and advised him not to order anything too expensive."

Mike described how he had placed second in the state cross country meet last November and was looking to improve his performance in the distance events at next spring's track season. When Adam asked him about what he wanted to study in college, Mike replied that he wasn't sure just yet. "I'm thinking about physical therapy or something in the medical field. Maybe I'll go pre-med if my grades are good enough. Anything but pre-law." That last statement wounded Adam but he suppressed any instinct to shoot back with some stinging response and said simply that all of those were good options. "Well, I've got to be going, Dad."

"Did you see Adam gritting his teeth when Mike said 'Anything but pre-law'? Then when his son left, Adam exhaled as if he were saying 'I guess I deserved that response.' Maybe Adam can learn something from this experience," Amanda concluded.

"He should be grateful that he's not staring Death in the face and may still have time to make things better," Carrie added.

Adam's visit with his daughter Cassie didn't go any better. Adam had to wait for the January storm to pass before he set out on the three hour drive to visit his daughter at her college. He hoped and—unusual for Adam—prayed that his old rust bucket of a car could make the trip. Even gas money presented a problem.

But from the outset, the trip was a disaster. True, Adam had saved up enough money to pay for gas and to take Cassie out to a moderately priced restaurant—she had spoken of a place she liked—but his savings would pay for the trip only if everything went perfectly. They didn't. He woke to a frigid cold January morning with temperatures in the single digits. His car wouldn't start. From that frustrating mechanical sound, he knew it was the battery. He had let his road service lapse, so he had no choice other than to trudge the four blocks to the Tire and Battery place down the street. "I shouldda known this would happen," Adam mumbled. So, he wrapped up the old battery in some old rags that were lying in the garage and started on his way. He kept looking up at the sky, fearful that the snow would start falling. It didn't, but the threat alone harried Adam. He had other concerns. All the money that he had reserved for the restaurant bill and any incidental expenses vanished into the cash register of the Tire and Battery place. He had no choice other than to pay cash. His credit cards were maxed out and he was making minimal payments all the while incurring maximum interest charges. He trudged back home, installed the battery, and called Cassie to tell her that he would be late because of car trouble. Then he realized a fateful irony. "Hell, I used that old excuse about car trouble on more than one occasion when I was playing around during the time I should have been visiting the kids. Yeah, as they say, what comes around goes around. And I'm at the bottom end of that trajectory, the shit hole end."

Adam finally arrived two hours late only to be greeted by another disappointment. "Dad, I've got a physics lab in forty-five minutes and I can't be late for it."

"I understand. Studies first. Well, I guess I'll settle for a rain check on the lunch date. How about an ice cream?"

From above, Amanda commented. "I'll bet he's just as relieved as he is disappointed. Now he won't have to invent an excuse for not being able to pay for a restaurant bill. And you know what? When he asked his daughter about an ice cream, I'll wager that he felt like a fool. Did you see him blush ever so faintly? He hasn't had any interaction with Cassie for years and doesn't know how to act around her. In fact, in a lot of ways, he doesn't know how to interact with women, period."

The short walk over to the Dairy Queen resembled a Death March. Disappointed with himself and not knowing what to say or how to act around his daughter, Adam hung his head low as the icy wind roared past. Just at he time he was hoping to succeed as a father, he had failed—or thought he had.

Cassie seemed slightly amused at the whole episode. She walked briskly ahead, two paces, then three, then four ahead of her father. She ordered a single scoop ice cream cone, as did her father. They talked briefly about the weather and her studies, and then she left for her physics lab. Adam sat alone. Not many people ordered ice cream on a blustery day in January. Then he walked over to his car, hoped it would start, and headed home to his empty mansion.

INVOKING THE DEAD

J ANUARY YIELDED TO FEBRUARY. THE oak leaves that had survived the first onslaught of winter had finally succumbed to the cold and dark. They fluttered down or were blown around by the winter winds. Even the scrub growth of wild bushes had been scrubbed clean.

"Humans confound me," Amanda remarked as she gazed down at the sight beneath her. "They pride themselves on being rational beings, so much above the rest of the animate and sentient creatures that they lord it over the rest of us, and yet they have such irrational customs and practices. Look at the month of February. For some reason or other it is shorter than the rest, only twenty- eight days. And the humans frequently forget to pronounce the r and say *Febuary* and not *February*. They can be most irrational even as they boast of being so much superior to the rest of creation. They are a mass of contradictions, these humans."

"You're right, Amanda. Look below and what do you see?"

"On most February days a grey sky overlooks masses of brown—decaying leaves, rotting tree trunks lying in pools of water, nothing but drab colors everywhere. If any snow brightens the landscape, it is soon capped with all types of detritus—crumbled, decaying leaves, dirt, small bits of rotting twigs—and, in cities, engine oil and other grime, making the whole scene look soiled and dirty and trashy."

"Is it any wonder that the humans make it the shortest month of the year?" I asked rhetorically.

"All right, Phil," you've got me there. But what about the weird spelling? I mean, what's with the r in *February*?"

"A lot of human practices and customs and traditions result from

125

the mutations, permutations, and sometimes pure chaos of their history. Take spelling in English, for example. And it's not just *February*. What about the *k* sound in *knight* or *knife*? At one time the *k* sound was pronounced. But it's really tough to say the *k* sound and the *n* sound right after each other, so after time the *k* sound dropped."

"But why was there that troublesome *r* sound in the first place, Phil?"

"The month derives its name from the ancient Roman purification ritual, *Februum*. The ritual entailed sacrifices to the god of the dead."

Here Carrie broke in. "By February any food left from the autumn harvest is gone. There's no fodder for the grazing animals to feed on except dead brown grass and broadleaf plants. So, many animals die in late winter and early spring. For humans, February meant famine; for us vultures, it meant feast. It's the way of Nature. As some suffer and perish, others fatten and thrive."

"Look at the scene below us," I commented, as it was time to return to our task. "What do you see?"

Adam was tottering about like an old man, still only half-awake. He almost stumbled into the bathroom, supported himself with both arms, and then gazed into the mirror. What he saw must have shocked him. "My God, what has become of me?" His beard was grizzled, his hair turning as grey as the low-lying clouds above him, bluish-black pools lay beneath his eyes. He had started to lose weight as the skin sagged on his upper arms—no muscle or fat to fill it out. He was beginning to look like a balloon slowly losing air.

"Hell, I've got to start doing something. In less than thirty days, I'll have my law license back. Now it's time to start writing those letters, making those contacts, setting up interviews. I'm out of money. I can't let myself be out of luck as well. I can't let my kids see me this way."

Amanda couldn't resist the temptation to comment. "Well, at least he's thinking about someone else other than himself although he's more concerned with his appearance than anything else. Maybe there's a faint glimmer of hope for the old guy, after all."

So, Adam threw himself into a flurry of letter writing. First he wrote and left a telephone message for the firm where he had begun his career before he ventured out on his own. He checked the website of

McWaters & Knight thoroughly before he composed his letter. "The old man is dead," Adam muttered, "and his son has taken over. Not a good sign. The son and I started out just two years apart and I had always outshone him, charging far more billable hours and winning far more cases and settlements. Well, if I come hat in hand, verging on begging, maybe he'll consider it my comeuppance. The old wheel of Fortune just keeps turning and right now I'm on the bottom and the old man's son is at the top." So, Adam weighed his words most carefully or so it seemed from all of the pauses and rewrites and revisions upon revisions. I had witnessed Adam dashing off letters in a few minutes, even ones longer than one page, but now he labored over each word and strained to communicate just the right tone and message. "I've got to establish my competence and my repentance or at least the appearance of the latter," Adam said, trying to convince himself of the power of every word. Finally, after two hours, he mailed the letter. By now it was 9:30 am and Adam felt he could leave a phone message with McWaters, Jr. He didn't anticipate instant results, so he devoted the next three days almost in their entirety to writing query letters to forty different law firms in the metropolitan area. Writing these letters proved easier than his first efforts to re-establish himself professionally. On the fourth day, he received a telephone call from Mr. McWaters' secretary, asking him if he could show up at ten o'clock the next morning for an interview. "This is it. I've got the old mojo back," Adam exclaimed.

That night Adam couldn't sleep as he rehearsed answers to every conceivable question about civil law. "I pulled all-nighters in law school, so it's no big deal," he boasted, but no one else heard him except for himself and me and my two colleagues. He had forgotten that he had aged. He showed up for the interview looking wan and weak, his eyes floating deep bluish-purple pools. The secretary greeted him professionally and coldly. "Take a seat, Mr. Albright. Mr. McWaters will call you in momentarily." Adam dutifully followed the orders. Glancing at the clock, he noticed that it slipping past 9:30. Soon it was 9:45 and Adam almost squirmed in his seat. By 10:00, Adam rose and started to head towards the exit, but the secretary called him back. "Mr. McWaters will see you now, Mr. Albright."

Adam knocked twice and paused, waiting for a response. After a few seconds, he heard a gruff, "Come in." Adam opened the door slowly, took three strides in, and halted one foot away from the edge of the large gleaming cherry wood table. His former colleague had papers in front of him—papers so important that he never took his eyes off them. He didn't offer his hand and appeared utterly disinterested. Finally, he paused from his study of whatever lay in front of him and said, "So, you'd like your old job back come March. Is that right, Adam?"

"Yes, Sir, I'd be delighted to work again for the first firm that took me in and tutored me professionally."

"Well, you didn't learn everything from us, now did you?"

"No, Sir, but I've learned from my mistakes and am ready to start over again."

"Start over, huh? Well, we don't have any junior openings just now and generally we're looking after bright young, and ethical candidates fresh out of law school. I called you in as a favor to a former colleague. Take my advice and look for something new. Remake yourself. That's all. My secretary will show you out."

"I can find my own way," Adam retorted. As he raced down the hallway to the elevators that would drop him ten flights below, Adam muttered. "The son of a bitch just called me in to humiliate me and lord it over me. I'll bet he really got his jollies telling me to 'Remake yourself.' Hell, I've got thirty-nine more applications out, and one of them will pan out. Then I can go tell McWaters, Jr., to remake himself."

Amanda shook her head and then her whole body. "I don't think any of Adams's letters will result in a job or even an interview. He's a persona non grata, right, Phil."

"Yes, Amanda, you're right. But Adam ought to reconsider the advice to remake himself. Oh, I know that those words just resonated with smug paternalism. But in a way McWaters didn't imagine, he's right. The old self has died and Adam must find a new self."

For the next week, Adam rushed out to the mailbox and listened to telephone messages. At first the mailbox contained nothing but bills, but then responses to his query letters came out. He tore the first few open ravenously, but they all contained the same message: a form-letter rejection notice. The telephone calls all consisted of robo-calls, soliciting contributions for this or that political candidate. The ones asking for donations to Senator Wainwright's treasure chest proved particularly galling. He had failed.

From on high Carrie soared and roared from above. "Adam's old self must die and he must remake himself anew."

Carrie's words must have thundered down to Adam, for he was remaking himself in at least one way. He still paid his child support but not grudgingly as he had in the past but willingly, even enthusiastically. Even though Adam had little money, he still set aside enough each month to fulfill his duty. He started calling his children twice weekly. He attended one of his son's indoor track meets and applauded him at every turn. And that meant that he applauded often. Adam ran a 3,000 meter race on a two hundred meter track so the turns came often as the athletes whizzed by. He and Mike talked of future plans. Mike still wanted to race at the collegiate level, but track and cross country scholarships were few. He'd have to place in the top two or three at the state meet to even be considered for a scholarship to a Division I or even II school. "Could run at a Division III school, but there'd be no athletic scholarship. I already have an academic partial scholarship to a local Division III school. Cassie told me to take the academic scholarship and run and enjoy myself. She told me I'm not going to run professionally, and Division I athletes at her school don't have a scholarship; they have a job. What do you think, Dad?"

"I think your older sister is wise beyond her years." Adam managed another trip to see his daughter but had no pretenses—or money—for a restaurant meal. Because he wasn't sure his old heap of a car would make the trip, he took the bus. He had no grandiose plans. Instead they talked quietly over a cup of coffee in the student lounge.

"You know that Mom's getting remarried, Dad."

"I wish her the best. She deserves as much happiness as possible."

"You're so generous, Dad." Cassie kissed him on the forehead and the two hugged even in the public space of the student lounge. When Adam rose to leave and had walked far enough away so that his daughter couldn't see him, he exhaled ever so slowly as if regretting what might have been.

"Maybe there's some hope for Adam, after all," Amanda concluded.

MARCHING TO VICTORY, SORT OF

"**S**O, NOW IT'S MARCH. ADAM has his law license restored but no job. Phil, as you would volunteer to explain anyway, what does the month of March portend for old Adam?" Amanda looked resigned to another one of my explanations stocked full of antiquarian lore.

"Well, March derives its name from the Roman god of war, Mars. In English, there's a kind of pun on the name of the month and on marching off to battle. The Romans and other peoples of antiquity campaigned from March through November and then took up winter quarters."

Somewhat intrigued, Amanda then said, "Why wouldn't they fight each other during the winter? It's not as if the aggression-gene suddenly stopped working and all were living in peace and harmony. January seems just as good as June for throwing stones on those catapult things and shooting arrows and tossing javelins and crossing swords and doing all those types of bloody things humans do to each other."

"Sometimes the ancients did attack during the winter but then mostly on a much smaller scale, more like raids rather than battles so the body counts were lower. They holed up in the winter because there was no fodder for their oxen, horses, and other beasts of burden. One of the human grandmasters of warfare claimed that an army travels on its belly. Often times logistics, not battlefield strategy wins the day."

"I guess that humans can pat themselves on the back now that mechanized warfare can let them slaughter each other throughout the year. Well, anyway, Phil, you still haven't answered my question about what does March portend for old Adam?"

"True, I do indulge myself in all manner of antiquarian lore now that I have an eternity to do so. Well, Adam isn't literally going off to battle, but he is engaging the enemy—which in this case is poverty. He's got to secure a job to feed himself. It won't be easy to do so, not with his reputation anyway."

"Look at him, Phil, he's racing to the mailbox only to rip open a succession of rejection letters. Then he tosses them into a box after checking off the name of each firm that's rejected him. He hasn't even had an interview since that first one. What's he going to do?"

Down on earth, Adam wasn't dealing well with all of the failures. He was used to success. He tried to drink himself into oblivion but even that failed. He tossed the cheap booze aside as it burned him going down. "I guess I can sell the mansion. It's almost spring and people will be looking to buy now. What the hell, what good is a mansion if I live in only three rooms anyway? I can't afford to heat the rest. Hell, come next December, I won't be able to pay the real estate taxes. What the hell, I was getting sick of doing all that yard work anyway." He went to a realtor, signed a contract, and that was it. He was selling his place "As Is," he told the realtor because he couldn't afford to do the repairs. While that reality pained him, he felt even more distress about the fact that the money from selling his Beemer had long since run out. He had no job and no prospect of a job. "Maybe I need to expand my horizons in this job search thing." On a walk through the park, the same one that in the autumn had seen him leading the rallies for Senator Wainwright, he picked up a newspaper that someone had discarded on a park bench. "Who reads newspapers anymore? It's all on the internet." Nevertheless, he picked p the printed version of the news and began reading it eagerly. He came to the "Help Wanted" section and saw in a box: "Legal Aid needs lawyers, full or part-time. Call for an appointment."

He called the number while still sitting on the bench. "Hello, I'm Adam Albright. I'm calling about the position for a lawyer with Legal Aid."

For a painful few moments, dead silence reigned supreme. Then a voice, slow and regretful, in carefully measured tones responded. "Yes, Mr. Albright, we know all about you." Adam sensed immediately what that response boded. They would hire him because they were desperate, but they didn't like the idea, not at all. "Can you come by our office this afternoon at 12:30?"

Somewhat too eagerly, Adam responded, "Yes, I'll be there." He raced home, showered again and even shaved again, took out his best suit, and carried with him his Vita, and placed it securely in an attaché case he hadn't used in decades. "My parents gave me that when I graduated from law school," he reflected. "They were so proud of me and my accomplishments. I wonder what they would think of me now."

Adam showed up ten minutes early for the appointment. He would have been fifteen minutes early, but he walked around the block, reasoning that "Ten minutes early creates a good impression of punctuality; fifteen minutes early shows desperation."

A voice from the lone private office in the space called him in. The voice didn't even extend a hand in greeting nor did it allow him to sit down. "I assume you've brought your Vita with you along with unofficial transcripts of you undergraduate and law school grades and your standing with the state bar. Put them down. We'll check them out later. Right now, we're swamped with work. So, here's our compensation package. It's not what you're used to, but it is what we can afford. Full-time employees get health care coverage after sixty days on the job. Here's your first case. Find a spot out on the table and get to work. There are a couple of laptop computers out there as well. We don't want our lawyers using their personal computers for their work, understand?" Adam nodded. "We like to keep public affairs and private ones separate. Of course, you can do legal research on your own computer, but all correspondence and legal papers are to be done on our computers."

Adam replied, "I understand." He knew what the voice on the other side of the desk was implying. As the Voice looked down on a stack of papers, Adam also realized that this action was the cue that told him to leave, sign the paper work, and then get to work. He picked up a file that apparently contained only a few pages.

When Adam found a vacant spot on the table outside that lone private office, he sat down and skimmed over the compensation package. He would be making a little less than what he made when he first started out and that was decades ago, but he would be getting a paycheck. He also knew that he had to have health insurance. He had weathered the past winter with only a few colds, but he knew that he had lucked out. "I'm not getting any younger," he reminded himself. Then he opened the file of his first case.

A middle-aged man sat down on the chair next to Adam. "You're new here, right?"

"Yes" was Adam's curt reply.

"You're that Albright guy, right?"

"Right again."

"I'll bet this was just about the only job you could get, right?"

Adam paused a little bit, clearly annoyed. "I've got to get to work, you know, and earn my paycheck."

"Hell, you don't have to worry about that. Just about everyone we represent here is guilty of something. It's all a matter of plea bargains and Alfred pleas. We try to get our clients off with as little time as possible. You get what I mean?"

"I hear you. But there's just one issue. I like to win."

"Have it your way, Adam." Then the man got up and left to pour himself a cup of coffee.

Adam read and re-read the file in front of him. He focused so intently that his eyes seemed to burn through the text. I knew I couldn't count on him reading any of the text out loud, so I invoked a little supernatural privilege and peered over his shoulder. A certain Antonio X was accused of assault and armed robbery. The victim of the crime would have evoked pity from even the most hardened of felons. She was an elderly lady, eighty-three years old in poor health. All of the neighborhood children called her Gramma as she frequently carried extra candy when she went out on her neighborhood strolls. I guess that *strolls* wouldn't be the right term, for she walked slowly and deliberately, partially supporting herself with a cane. Her assailant kicked the cane out of her hands and pushed her to the ground and threatened her with a knife. He yanked her purse from left hand and rifled through it until he found some cash and ran off with it. The woman remained frazzled and upset when the police arrived simultaneously with the ambulance. She declined any medical attention. She couldn't provide much of a description other than her attacker was slightly below average height, perhaps 5' 7" or 5'6", medium build, with light complexion. The officer on the scene apparently said something like, "Well, that fits about thirty people in this neighborhood." Two hours later, a young man fitting that description was walking in the neighborhood and one woman Maria Delores, called in, saying that she didn't get that good of a look at Gramma's assailant, but she thought that she might have seen him just walking by. The police arrived and she pointed to the four family flat, where the suspect had entered apartment 2-A. When the police arrived, they questioned the suspect, Antonio X about his whereabouts two hours ago. He wouldn't answer the question, so the police arrested him and charged him with the attack. Because of the brutal nature of the attack, Antonio X was still being held in jail, pending a trial.

After reading and rereading the account, Adam finally broke his silence and muttered out loud. "Something isn't right here."

"I think Adam figured that if Antonio was guilty he would have given a phony alibi and had some of his friends cover for him," Amanda declared.

"I think you're on to something, Amanda, although his refusal to tell the police where he was when the assault took place doesn't look good for him," I countered.

"He's trying to protect someone," Carrie added, "although I don't know who."

Adam checked out of the office and visited Antonio in jail, something he had never done in his entire career. When Adam asked him why he wouldn't state where he had been during the crime, he just sat with his arms folded and glared at no one in particular. "Look, Antonio," Adam said as objectively as he could, "I can't offer much of a defense if you won't talk." Still no response. So, Adam scrawled his name and phone number on a piece of paper he had ripped from his yellow legal pad. "All right, here's my name and phone number if you decide to change your mind." Adam got up slowly, hoping that Antonio would respond. He didn't. He just continued to sit with his arms folded, glaring at the world.

That night, Adam managed to do a crash course in criminal law and judicial proceedings, something he hadn't done since his law school days decades ago. In the morning, he walked into the office unsure of his abilities but sure of one thing. He hoped that Antonio had left him a message. He hadn't. But a young woman named Mercedes had. One of the law students staffing the Legal Aid office handed Adam the message. "Antonio was with me when that nice old lady was attacked. We were at the motel something, midtown. It's on Pine Street if that helps. Anyway, don't tell my mother. She would kill me if she found out I was there. Anyways check it out with the motel clerk. We were there and Antonio registered, using his own name. At least, that's what he told me. I stayed in the car until he got a room for us, so the clerk might not know about me, but he did kind of snicker when Antonio paid for the room in cash. I could see him through the window. He was that obvious. Don't believe me. Check it out for yourself."

Adam did. His hooptie rolled into the parking lot of the motel along with a few other cars in the same condition. He asked the clerk if he could take a look at the register from last week. "And just why would you want to do that? Checking on the old lady?"

"No, I'm not married. Look all want to know is a young guy named Antonio X was here last week and when he was here."

"What's the big deal? You don't look like his father."

"So, he was here? I'm his lawyer."

"Hey, I don't want nothing to do with no lawyer."

"Would it help if I told you that I'm defending him against an assault charge."

"So, why don't you ask the pretty little lady who was with him?"

"The prosecutor would be more likely to believe his alibi if it came from an objective source."

"Yeah, I see your point, but I don't want nothing to do with no court case. I don't keep a fancy register or anything. For the guys who pay with a credit card, there's no problem. I got the copy of the receipt. But, if I don't know them, guys who pay in cash got to sign in and show some ID. I mean, I got to know who to go after. You wouldn't believe it, but sometimes either just wreck the place or steal me blind. About six months ago, some guy comes, pays cash, and stays overnight, and then takes off with all the bedding—pillows, covers, sheets, you name it. I don't run a Bed, Bath & Beyond, you know. You just wouldn't believe what goes on around here."

"Oh, I believe it, all right. But how about if I just take a photo of the register and just the entry for Antonio. That might be enough to persuade the distract attorney to drop the charges."

"And if it ain't?"

"I'll still try to keep you out of it."

"Yeah, all right. That Antonio guy was no pro at the dating game, if you know what I mean. I mean he was shaking and all when he registered."

"Thanks," then Adam took off and met with one of the assistant DA's assigned to Antonio's case. "Look, Adam, you're going to need more than that grainy photo snapped from a seedy motel's register. I'm surprised that they're still asking for guests to sign in."

"Only when they pay in cash," Adam responded. "Otherwise, they just use the credit card receipt."

"Yeah, well, at least that makes a little sense. Look I'm not about to release Antonio just yet, but I will offer you this. The victim has recovered enough that she volunteered to do a line-up. If she ID's Antonio as the assailant, he's toast. Otherwise, we go to look for someone else. Look, the neighborhood is pushing us on this matter. Everyone liked and loved Gramma. We need to get this case off our plate."

The line-up was scheduled for the next day. Apparently it didn't take too much time to get five men who fit the description. As the police officer stated in the notes that Adam read, there must have been thirty guys who fit the general description of the perp. "Oh, they all look so much alike," Gramma said as she viewed the young men in the line-up. "But as I look closer, one detail stands out. I'm remembering it now. Yes, I can see it. When I was pushed down, I stared into his face and I saw one thing that I remember now clear as day. The man who attacked me had three tear drops tattooed, I guess, below his right eye." Adam breathed a sigh of relief. Antonio had no such markings.

"At least now we know who did it," one officer said. "It's gotta be Darren Jackson. He's got quite a rep in the neighborhood and one hell of a long rap sheet. We'll bring him in and see what he was doing when old Gramma got attacked."

When Antonio was released, he insisted on seeing Adam. "I gotta at least thank the guy." Antonio walked up to Adam and looked him in the eye. "Thanks, you didn't say anything about Mercedes, did you?"

"No I tried to keep her out of it."

"Yeah, well, thanks again."

When Adam checked back in at the Legal Aid office, he was told to report to the private office of Mr. Weidman. Since there was only one private office there, he knew where to go.

"I'll bet he's afraid he'll get fired but is puzzled why," Amanda observed from on high.

"Sometimes, there's just no justice," Carrie added.

I wasn't so sure—at least not this time. Still, when Adam knocked twice on the door to Mr. Weidman's office, I could see him exhale and swallow hard.

"Sit down, Adam." Mr. Weidman said as he stood up and greeted Adam. "I guess I figured you wrong. I was afraid that all you'd do was argue for a pleas bargain and that would be it. We don't get that many wins in this business so we celebrate every one we get. Congratulations, Adam. You're off to a great start. Just keep it up. Here's your next case." Adam took the file enthusiastically. "Just don't take too long basking in your glory. We've got a lot of cases here."

This new case involved a civil matter: a wrongful termination of employment. When Adam sat down on the table outside Mr. Weidman's office, the same fellow who talked briefly with him before sat three feet away, slowly sipping from an over-sized coffee cup. Other attorneys, interns, and volunteers were either bustling about or, like Adam, intently focused on the papers before them or busily tapping away at one of the office's laptops. Still, Adam paused long enough to look at the man beside him. He had longish, grey hair that curled around in tangles on every side and overlapped his ears. He wore a crumpled white shirt and a blue tie with a few random yellow stains scattered here and there in drooping little droplets. I couldn't tell for sure, but I think they were the remnants of egg yolks. Then the man with the spotted tie spoke. "Hey, what the hell, you trying to make the rest of us look bad?"

Adam briefly turned towards him with a puzzled look. "What are you talking about?"

"Winning that first case."

"That was just the luck of the draw. The man was innocent."

"Yeah, right. They all are."

Adam returned to his close scrutiny of the next case, but before doing so scanned the room around him. Everywhere people were working hard: perusing a file like himself, or composing letters and other documents on laptops or taking the many calls that seemed to never end. He had had the misfortune to seat himself next to the one resident slacker. So, Adam ignored him and focused on the matter before him.

Once again, I had to invoke a little privilege and read over his shoulder. Mr. Weidman must have been playing some kind of joke on Adam. This civil case involving a wrongful termination of employment was all wrapped up in a sexual harassment matter. The plaintiff was suing her former supervisor for sexual harassment but didn't seek any money, just a public apology to clear her name. If the suit had involved a monetary claim for damages, it probably would have been handed off to any number of lawyers who will work for a share of the settlement; it wouldn't have been a matter for Legal Aid. In the file, the plaintiff, Victoria Gonzalez, named three other women who had also been pressured for sex. Adam called them up one by one, and one by one they gave the same response: yes, they were pressured but no they were afraid to go public for fear of losing their job. What compounded the matter was that two of the other three women were illegal immigrants who feared that they would be deported if they spoke up—at least that's what the supervisor, Mr. Ernesto Gutierrez, had told them. The three victims spoke to Adam on the condition of anonymity.

Adam made a phone call to Mr. Gutierrez and arranged to meet him the next morning at nine o'clock sharp. As he thought over what he was going to say, Adam mulled over his options on the way home. When he arrived, the temperature sat in the mid-thirties with a dark sky overhead pouring down a constant flow of bone-chilling rain. Nevertheless, Adam glowed with energy. "It's time to play a little poker and bluff," he declared.

The next morning, he dressed himself in his best suit and paid minute attention to every detail of dress. He even dug deep into his wallet and paid for a cab out of his own funds. Luckily, Mr. Gutierrez's office lay only a mile and a half away "I can't show up in my hooptie. I've got to be the vision of success in every way I can."

Adam arrived promptly at 8:55. Mr. Gutierrez's secretary notified her boss that Mr. Adam Albright was here for his nine o'clock appointment. "Tell him, I'll be with him momentarily." Adam had expected that response. As he sat, waiting, he also wondered if his secretary was one of his victims. She was young, perhaps nineteen or twenty, had glowing brown complexion, with perfectly manicured nails—just the type of victim someone like Mr. Gutierrez (or himself in the past) would have groomed to be his next bed mate of the moment. Adam stared at her nameplate: Dolores. Amanda and I talked it over. There was a Dolores mentioned in the complaint, but that is a relatively common name, so we both noticed. "Still," Amanda wagered, "I'll bet that she will be a factor in Adam's bluff."

"So, the two of them are going to play what the humans call a pissing contest, right, Phil?"

"Right you are, Amanda." I shot back. "And I bet old Adam will win."

At nine o'clock sharp, Mr. Gutierrez notified his secretary to let Mr. Albright in. Adam entered only to see Mr. Gutierrez leaning back in his chair and touching the tips of the fingers of each hand together. "Why don't you stop wasting your time, Mr. Albright? This is just a matter of one disgruntled employee trying to get back at her old boss: her word against mine, the word of a mere clerk against that of a successful businessman. The case will be tossed."

"What you say, Mr. Gutierrez is correct," Here Adam paused to allow Mr. Gutierrez to smirk. "However, I've got three other complainants, all of whom have similar tales to tell. Right now, Victoria is not pursuing any monetary claims. She wants only a public apology to clear her name in her community. As for the other three, I don't know."

"What other three?" Mr. Gutierrez demanded.

Adam said nothing in response, only turning his head and conspicuously fixing his eyes as if he were seeing through the door. "It's your choice, Mr. Gutierrez: apologize for what you could claim was a momentary lapse in judgment which will never occur again or risk losing every dime you've ever made."

139

Mr. Gutierrez looked down into his lap. "Only an apology, you say, for a lapse in judgment."

"And a vow to never act in such a manner again."

"All right, Mr. Albright, you've got my apology. I'll draft a letter and send it out by noon."

"Phil, did you leave something out?" Amanda asked.

I smiled. "Now what do you think I left out?"

"I'll bet that Adam felt confident in the bluff because he had read that Mr. Gutierrez was a married man who couldn't afford either an expensive law suit or an even more expensive divorce."

"Well," I responded. "You can't show all of your cards at once."

Despite the cold March rain, Adam walked the ten blocks back to the Legal Aid office. "Another win," he boasted as he strode down the sidewalk.

"Adam's still wrapped up in his sense of personal glory, but in these two cases maybe that isn't so bad. At least he's helping the needy out. There's nothing wrong with that kind of winning, I guess." Amanda turned her head aside as if still mulling over matters. "Yes, I suppose I'm getting to like him after all."

REDEFINING LOVE AND LIFE

I N EARLY APRIL, ADAM HAD reason to celebrate: his mansion had sold. "I guess my old life is gone," he said, but not regretfully. "I'll get a three-room apartment near the Legal Aid office and the park, the same park where he had held the rallies for Senator Wainwright. But whatever echoes of those old rallies had remained were long since gone. With the money from the sale of his house, Adam paid off his credit card debt, banked some money for emergencies, and invested the rest—but not in Let the Sun Shine In company. He'd let Senator Bobby do that. Then, as Adam pored over his finances, he exhaled and then admitted a reality that he had long overlooked. "I owe a lot to my children for all of the years that I wasn't a father to them. I can't really get those years back. I also can't buy their love. They've got every right to ignore me, maybe even hate me. Maybe I can make their lives a little bit better. I can send them each a check for $10,000 to pay for school, to reduce their student debt, to take a load off their shoulders. I hope and pray that they won't regard this gift as some kind of bribe, some way to buy their love. I guess I'll have to swallow some more pride and admit that I wasn't much of a husband to Mary, either. Maybe she'd know what to do."

Adam turned the idea over and over in his mind. He couldn't sleep all night. The next morning, though, he took a deep breath and called his former wife, but not before carefully rehearsing what he would have to say. Finally, after running through his script a dozen times, he made the call. "Hello, Mary, first of all I'd like to congratulate you on your wedding. I wish you and your future husband the best, and I mean that.

You deserve the best life you can have, and you couldn't have found that good life with me. As the mother of my children, you are the best person to advise me. If I gave each of them $10,000, would either one or both view it as a bribe, as some kind of way to buy their love at the last hour? I want to do something for them, and I can't buy back the lost years. I also don't want to interfere with their relationship with you and their future stepfather. I can wait and defer the gift if you think that's a good idea. But I do want to do something. What do you think?"

Silence reigned supreme for a few moments. Then Mary spoke in slow, measured tones. She, too, knew she was treading on slippery grounds. "I'm flabbergasted, Adam. I never expected this of you. You always paid child support on time, but then again you always paid your electric bills on time, too. Once Cassie graduated from high school, you also paid half of her tuition at the state university. You never broke the settlement, didn't even bend it. For that, I'm grateful. Why do you want to give them more now as a gift, not as an obligation?"

"I sold the old mansion and have money sitting around that I would only blow on stuff and experiences I don't need and that wouldn't do me any good. So, I'm really doing this for myself."

"Whatever you say, Adam." Here Mary paused as if she needed time to wade through a torrent of ideas flowing through her mind. "What do you say to this proposal? You put the money in an account for each of them and one that they can't draw from until they graduate from college and have a job. Then each of them can determine how to spend the money: pay off student loans, buy a good used car, maybe save it as a down payment on a house, but no extravagant vacations or luxury cars, just the basics. You can stipulate all of that in some kind of trust, can't you?"

"Yes, and I won't bill any of you for the hours it'll take to do just that."

"You're kidding, right?"

"Yeah, I've become quite a jokester in my old age."

"And I am talking to Adam Albright, right?"

"Right again."

"All right, then we're set. I'll tell the children about the arrangement if you don't mind. I think it's important that they view this decision

142

as a joint one. I'll be sure to let them know that the money is coming from you."

"Right yet again. Best wishes on your wedding. I'll arrange the trust and let you talk about it with our children."

They both hung up the phone at the same time. "Why did it take me so long for me to value what I should have valued and loved all along? I was playing the fool when I was playing around."

"You know, Phil, I think I'm beginning to like old Adam, the new, improved version, that is."

"So am I, Amanda," I responded. "He's a new person."

"No need for me to be around for a while," Carrie said as she flapped her wings and soared off into the heavens above.

"But, Phil, I do need to know one thing: what's the significance of the month of April?"

I think Amanda was asking me that question just to make me feel good about showing off some of knowledge. I have to admit that I was glad she asked me. "The month of April derives from the name of the Greek goddess Aphrodite, Venus in Latin. She is the goddess of love and fertility. It celebrates the rebirth of life following the dead of winter."

"But love has many meanings, does it not, Phil?"

"More than I can count, Amanda, but far too many stop at only one meaning—sex. Love has many forms as Adam is learning. By the way, Amanda, your own name comes from Latin and means 'one who deserves to be loved.'"

Printed in the United States
by Baker & Taylor Publisher Services